Fortress of the Dead

Chris Roberson

An Abaddon Books™ Publication
www.abaddonbooks.com
abaddon@rebellion.co.uk

This edition published in 2020 by Abaddon Books™,
Riverside House, Osney Mead, Oxford, OX2 0ES, UK.

Creative Director and CEO: Jason Kingsley
Chief Technical Officer: Chris Kingsley
Head of Books and Comics Publishing: Ben Smith
Deputy Publishing Manager: Rob Power
Editors: David Thomas Moore,
Michael Rowley and Kate Coe
Design: Sam Gretton, Oz Osborne and
Gemma Sheldrake

Zombie Army: Fortress of the Dead
Copyright © 2020 Rebellion.

ISBN: 978-1-78108-854-8

Printed in Denmark.

Fortress of the Dead

Chris Roberson

**ABADDON
BOOKS**

WWW.ABADDONBOOKS.COM

ZOMBIE ARMY

Fortress of the Dead

Chris Roberson

CHAPTER 1

THE VILLAGE MUST have had a name at some point, but it seemed there was no one left alive who remembered what it had been. Now it was a withered husk of a place, a few ramshackle buildings still standing and the rest just piles of rubble, marked down with a reference number and a set of coordinates in an old survey map that the squad had been issued at their last briefing. They'd been working their way across the map for the last three weeks, crossing off one reference number after another as they went, and this was the last spot on their list.

"Looks quiet to me," Jun said, peering through the scope of her T-99 bolt action at the ruins from half a mile south of the village.

"Isn't that what you said two days ago?" Sergeant Josiah said as Jun lowered her rifle.

"Yes, sir." Jun admitted, then spun the cap off

her canteen and took a long swig of lukewarm water, gazing north past the ruined village at the looming Alps which crowded the skies beyond.

"Well…" the sergeant added as he turned to her with a lopsided grin. "Those bastards *were* pretty quiet, I'll admit."

Jun rolled her eyes as she tightened the lid back on the canteen. Sure, the last village had been quiet enough, before a half-dozen Dead burst out of a burned out farmhouse right as the squad was passing by. One of the damned things almost managed to take a bite out of Sibyl before Jun put it down with a lucky headshot from her T-99.

"Okay, team, look alive." The sergeant slung the Springfield over his shoulder and motioned for the others to follow him in. "Let's get this one crossed off and we can head back to base camp and put our feet up for a bit."

"Maybe they'll even pin a medal on us," Curtis Goodwin muttered under his breath while rubbing the stubble on his narrow chin. "Hail the conquering heroes."

"Oh, cheer up," Sibyl Beaton scolded, and wagged a finger at the young American slouching along beside her. "It's like my Chester always used to say, a job well done is its own reward."

"Yeah?" Curtis glanced back over his shoulder

at Werner Sauer bringing up the rear. "Is that how you fellas handled things on your side of things back in the war? I seem to recall a fair number of German brass with a whole lot of hardware hanging off their chests."

"I think Frau Beaton is right, in essence." The German shrugged noncommittally. "One does one's duty. What else matters?"

Jun could see the ghost of a scowl flit across Sibyl's face, her jaw tightening momentarily, eyes narrowing darkly. In the next instant, Sibyl's features were as composed and placid as always, the proper Englishwoman once more. It was clear that Sibyl didn't much care for Werner, though whether it was simply because they so recently had fought on the opposite sides of the last war or because of something more personal, Jun didn't know.

"I ever tell y'all about the time I got a medal from the king of Siam himself, back in '41?" The sergeant grinned, and gave Jun a wink. "On account of me wrestling a pair of alligators that otherwise would have gobbled him up whole."

"Does Siam even have a king anymore, sarge?" Curtis rubbed the back of his neck, a quizzical expression on his face.

"Oh, don't spoil the fun, dear boy," Sibyl

answered with a sly smile. "Josiah is just spinning another of his tall tales, surely."

"In no particular order," Jun began, ticking off points on one finger at a time, "it hasn't been called 'Siam' since 1940, Thailand *does* have a king but he was a student in Switzerland after he was crowned in 1935, and I'm pretty sure that neither Thailand nor Switzerland has any alligators roaming free. So unless the sergeant was on a field trip to a zoo with the young king, I very much doubt that…"

"All right, all right, missy," the sergeant held his hands up in mock surrender. "So I misspoke."

Jun couldn't help but smile. To be able to stop just one of the sergeant's nonsensical yarns before it spun too far out of control was, in the words of Sibyl's late husband, its own reward.

"So maybe I misremembered, and it wasn't alligators," the sergeant corrected, "it was a pair of *crocodiles* I saved his majesty from, okay?"

Jun started to protest, but the sergeant held up one hand in a fist at shoulder height, motioning the squad to halt. He had a look on his face that was strictly business, but he snuck in a quick wink in Jun's direction before addressing the others.

"Y'all know the drill," he said as he unslung the 12-gauge shotgun that hung at his back and racked the pump to chamber a round. "House to house, and if you come across any Dead bastards...?"

"Put those bastards down," Jun and the others replied in unison, their traditional call-and-response, as they shouldered their rifles and switched to close-quarters arms.

Back on the Eastern Front she'd once had to fend off one of the Dead with nothing more than a hammer to hand, so the twenty rounds in Jun's Thompson submachine gun felt more than adequate for the task at hand. There were definitely advantages coming west and joining the Resistance.

"And if there are any survivors, sarge?" Curtis asked as the team fanned out through the ruined street.

"Won't be none," the sergeant answered, his voice low. "'Cause if there was?" He shook his head, his mouth twisted into a scowl.

Curtis didn't answer, but Jun could tell what he was thinking from the look on his face. If there *had* been any survivors in the village to begin with, there wouldn't be any more.

The way it had been explained to the squad in their briefing back at base camp, in the early days of the Dead War the village had been overrun, and the ground forces of the Resistance in that part of Italy were too outnumbered to be of much help to the town's residents. In the end a bombing run had been ordered and the zombies in the village were wiped out of existence with a sustained aerial bombardment, on the understanding that all of the living residents of the village had already fled or died at the hands of the Dead. But if by chance any of the villagers had somehow managed to survive to that point, maybe by holding up in an attic or locked in a closet somewhere…?

Jun looked around. There were scarcely any walls left standing in the village, and the few that were bore the brutal scars of the bombing and scorch marks from the firestorms that raged in the aftermath. If the rotting and dismembered bodies of the animated Dead could not survive that kind of inferno, it was impossible to imagine that a living person could make it through in one piece, either.

Still, there had been that time the previous week when Jun had been sure that a scuttling noise she heard from a barn was a group of Dead inadvertently trapped inside, only to find that it was actually the farmer and his family trying desperately to keep their only surviving sheep from alerting any passing Dead of their presence. If Jun had fired too fast, had acted on instinct rather than waiting and confirming her suspicions before acting, then the blood of that farmer or his wife or either of his two children might well have been on Jun's hands. And they would have been left buried in a mass grave along with the victims of the Dead, instead of transported safely to a secured compound to the south where the Resistance was safeguarding a growing population of survivors and refugees.

And if any of the villagers had still been alive when the Resistance's bombing run had begun, then their blood was on the hands of Jun's superior officers as well. The same people Jun had crossed a warzone to join, to help push back the Dead menace and protect the living—humanity's best chance of survival—would have been responsible for the death of the very innocents that they were charged with protecting.

It didn't bear dwelling on, Jun told herself. She knew that Curtis harbored his suspicions about similar aerial attacks on other Dead-infested villages and towns, as he voiced his concerns several times in recent weeks. In fact, Curtis had discussed it increasingly as they made through way across the Italian countryside checking on the villages marked in the old survey map as having been already cleared of Dead infestations, many of which had been subjected to bombing campaigns like the village they now found themselves in. They were ostensibly a deadhunter squad, but Curtis had insisted that they were really "batting cleanup," an Americanism he had used to describe their mission and that Jun hadn't really understood.

All Jun knew was that they had spent weeks going back over sites where battles against the zombies had already been won and making sure that ground had not been lost. And while it was important work, she was sure, it did sometimes feel more like they were groundskeepers making sure that pests had not gotten back into a garden than steely-eyed deadhunters out on the battleground protecting the living from the Dead. They did encounter the enemy from time to time, like the one that almost took a bite out of Sibyl in that village a couple of days earlier or the shambling horde they found in that silo the week before. But more often than not these villages and towns they were crossing off the survey map proved to be devoid of all interest and any threats, living or Dead.

"Anybody got anything?" the sergeant called from the other side of the road.

"Nein," Werner answered from the rear. "Nothing here."

Curtis just grunted, but Sibyl sang out, "Not a thing, Josiah, dear."

Jun shook her head when the sergeant looked

her way, but he arched an eyebrow and motioned for her to speak up.

"No movement here, sergeant," she answered. "But I wonder if maybe…"

Before she could continue her attention was snared by a sound right on the edge of hearing.

"Well?" The sergeant gave her a quizzical look.

"Hold on," Jun said in a quiet voice, and held up her hand for silence. "Do you hear that?"

There wasn't much to the nameless village but the one main road with the piles of rubble and the occasional freestanding wall to either side. To the south along the road, about a day's hike away, was situated the base camp from where their squad and other teams of deadhunters had been operating since they first moved into this part of Italy earlier in the year. To the north of the village the road cut back and forth as it travelled upland through the foothills of the Alps and presumably even higher. There had been no one and nothing on the road the way that they had come from the south, so where was the source of the sound that Jun was hearing…?

"There!" Werner was already slinging his MP40 over his shoulder and taking hold of his Karabiner 98K, changing up from close quarters to long range firing options. He brought the stock of his rifle to his shoulder, left eye squeezed shut and right eye narrowed as he peered through the scope at the distance. "Approaching from the north."

Jun spun around and looked in the direction Werner was facing, and sure enough, she could see movement on the road winding down out of the foothills towards them.

"Your orders, sergeant?" Werner asked, his finger hovering close to the trigger as he took sight.

Jun unslung her T-99 from her back to use its scope for a better look while the sergeant and the others followed suit. She counted ten, fifteen, maybe even as many as twenty bodies altogether, a frenzy of chaotic movement heading downhill towards the village. And a moment later another cluster of bodies following a short distance behind came into view around a bend in the road.

"I make two groups of hostiles, one following a few hundred yards behind the first," the sergeant said, surveying the scene.

"Orders?" Werner repeated.

Jun trained her sights on the forward most of the bodies rushing towards them. At the rate they were moving overland, they would reach the village in a matter of moments. But something about their movements seemed off to her.

"Pick your targets and fire on my command,"

the sergeant said.

It had been a while since they'd last run into a roaming horde of the Dead, but Jun could swear…

"Sir!" she shouted, lowering her rifle. "They're not hostiles!"

The sergeant's eye darted for the briefest moment in her direction, his eyebrow arched quizzically, and then he turned his attention back to his scope.

"Damn," the sergeant said under his breath after taking a closer look at the group hurrying downhill towards them. He could now clearly see what Jun had noticed; that the people rushing towards the village were living, breathing men and women, not the reanimated corpses of the enemy Dead. "Hold your fire, everyone. Looks like we've got another group of survivors on our hands."

"Something's got them pretty damned spooked, though," Curtis said, narrowing his gaze through his own scope.

The wind had shifted, and now they could more easily hear the shouts of alarm that had caught Jun's attention only moments before. And there was something else on the wind as well, a scent of death and decay that was all too familiar.

"Be a dear and take another look at the pack bringing up the rear, won't you, Josiah?" Sibyl's spoke in clipped syllables, the overt courtesy of her phrasing belying the urgency of her tone. "Quickly?"

The sergeant swung his rifle around and trained his scope on the second pack of bodies heading their way, and Jun did the same. It was difficult to see past the group in front, whose expressions of terror and exhaustion were now clearly visible through Jun's scope, but as the forward-most group descended a steep rise in the road the group behind them momentarily came into view.

"Just when I thought we were going to have a relaxing day of it," the sergeant sighed, just as the group in front once more obscured the bodies behind them from view.

The group in the rear were most definitely hostiles, a group of a dozen or more Dead wearing the tattered remnants of SS uniforms. They were not simply following the group of survivors heading down out of the foothills: they were *pursuing* them. The screaming mass of living men and women racing towards the nameless village were fleeing in terror from a squad of the Dead.

The deadhunter squad was the only hope that the fleeing survivors had of escaping imminent doom, but Jun and the others couldn't open fire on the pursuing Dead without running the risk of hitting the survivors with an errant shot.

"Orders?" Werner repeated.

"You, Curtis, and Sibyl get to higher ground and start taking out those Dead bastards at range as soon as you've got a clear shot." The sergeant slung his rifle on his back and took hold of his 12-gauge shotgun. "Jun, you're with me."

"What's the plan?" Jun asked.

"Come on!" Sergeant Josiah took off running directly for the approaching mass of bodies, and motioned urgently for Jun to follow along. "Let's go put those bastards down!"

CHAPTER 2

HEADSHOTS WERE BEST.

Jun had first learned to shoot a rifle on the Eastern Front, where she'd been serving as an attaché to a Chinese diplomat when Hitler activated Plan Z. She had joined the other surviving member of the delegation in defending the embassy, and she'd quickly understood that sniping at the Dead at long range with a rifle was far preferable to dealing with them in close quarters. And the Dead had the annoying and extremely dangerous habit of shrugging off anything but a clean headshot, and potting one with several shots in a row dead in their center mass wouldn't do much more than slow them down for a second or two. Jun had seen Dead with both legs and most of both arms blown off still dragging themselves across the ground towards their intended victims, jaws working furiously with a ravenous hunger for the flesh of the living. She'd even seen a headless Dead flop along for longer than expected after going down, but without a mouth to bite and chew they were more a curiosity than a real threat.

During Jun's time on the Eastern Front there were times when the ammunition ran short, and they'd had to resort to close-quarters fighting with the invading hordes of the Dead. And while an axe to the head usually did the trick as well as a sniper's bullet, there was the chance that the axe might get stuck in the skull while a still-shambling Dead attacked from another direction, so you always had to be careful to be mindful of other potential threats in close range. Aim all of your shots, hits, and strikes at the enemy's head, keep scanning for incoming, and never stop moving.

Jun could feel those old familiar instincts kicking into gear as she and the sergeant raced towards the panicked horde of survivors racing down the road.

"Move aside!" the sergeant shouted in English.

The survivors were replying in a babble of voices in a confusion of languages and accents, and Jun mostly just got the sense of panic and fear. And for the briefest of instants it appeared that the survivors thought that she and the sergeant were intending to attack *them*, fearfully eying the sergeant's pump-action shotgun and Jun's own Thompson submachine gun. Their fear of the Dead pursuing them was clearly greater, as they hardly slowed down, a few of them shouting out "Don't shoot" in heavily accented English.

"Out of the *way*!" the sergeant shouted, and then repeated similar sentiments in Italian, French, and German, waving his hand in a sharp gesture as if sweeping something ahead of him aside.

Understanding dawned on the terrified faces of the survivors, who immediately dove to either side just as the sergeant barreled through their ranks.

"Go on to the village," Jun said to the survivors as she passed by, and turned and pointed back the way that they'd come. "We'll hold them off."

She wasn't sure how many of the survivors understood what she was saying, but it seemed that her intent was clear enough. As she caught up with the sergeant, Jun chanced a quick glance over her shoulder, and saw that the survivors were already continuing down the road towards the ruined village.

"You sweep left, I'll go right," the sergeant shouted over to Jun as he skidded to a halt on the side of the road. The descending horde of Dead were only seconds away from reaching them.

"Yes, sir!" Jun raised her T-99 to her shoulder as she took up position across the road from the sergeant, and without hesitating fired a round into the head of the Dead leading the pack. The skull blew apart in an expanding bloom of bone fragments and gore, and as the headless body pitched forward Jun shifted her aim to the next Dead over, lined up her sights, and fired again.

It had been difficult to gauge the size of the Dead from the village below: Jun had originally thought they numbered around a dozen. But seen closer to, it was clear that there were more than that: many, many more. The rise and bend of the road had hidden their numbers, and what had originally seemed as little as a dozen was clearly more like two dozen, or even three. This was no small band of shamblers, but a considerable horde.

"Sergeant?" Jun said without taking her eyes off the targets, picking off another approaching Dead with a shot to the head. The falling bodies were slowing down the approaching horde somewhat, but it would not be much longer before the two of them were surrounded. She slung her T-99 over her shoulder and unslung her Thompson submachine gun, better suited for close quarters combat, and opened fire.

"Form up!" the sergeant shouted back, firing a

round from his shotgun that ripped through the head and torso of one of the Dead on his side of the road, racking the pump to chamber another round, then firing again at the next Dead over. "We hold this spot to give the survivors time to get clear."

Jun just nodded as she slid over to stand at the sergeant's side, firing short bursts from the Thompson into first one and then another of the Dead as she did, the hail of bullets sending bone fragments and rotting brain matter flying as their skulls burst like overripe melons.

The Dead were scrambling over the bodies of their fallen fellows now, spilling to the left and right sides of the road like a surging tide, hands out and grasping towards Jun and the sergeant, their jaws working furiously in their ruined mouths. But at least they seemed to have drawn the attention of the Dead away from the fleeing civilians, as the shambling horde appeared intent on devouring the two of them before continuing after the survivors still racing downhill towards the village.

"Sergeant?" Jun picked off another of the Dead who was circling around to their left, and so far they'd been able to keep all of the approaching horde on the uphill side of the road. But if they put it off much longer then the tide would spill all the way around them and they'd be surrounded.

"If they close around us, we'll take them back to back," the sergeant answered. His shotgun appeared to jam, and without missing a beat he drew his Colt M1911 from the holster at his belt and fired a single round into the eye socket of a Dead that had come almost within arm's reach. The Dead collapsed like a marionette whose strings had just been cut, the back of its skull exploding outwards and covering the other Dead coming up behind it with bits of rotted grey matter and fetid blood the color of India ink. "The important thing is to keep them back while those survivors get to cover."

Jun and the Sergeant were practically back to back as it was, but she didn't see anything to be gained from debating the point with him. She'd been given her orders, and it was her duty to carry them out.

"Bastard!" the sergeant shouted. He'd managed to clear the jammed shell that was lodged in his shotgun's ejection port, but barely had time to rack the action to chamber another round before one of the Dead was upon him. As it was when he fired the round that brought the Dead down it was at practically point blank range, and the resulting carnage was even more dramatic than usual.

Jun swore in Mandarin, scowling with fury.

She had tried to fire a round at another of the encroaching Dead but the Thompson's magazine drum was empty. There was another full drum hanging in a web of netting at her back, but she'd need a moment's grace to switch them out.

"Sergeant, can you cover me...?" Jun began, but the sergeant cut her off with a grunt before she could continue.

"Kind of got my hands full here, kid," the sergeant answered, taking out another Dead who had gotten so close that its clawing hand had ripped through the fabric of the sergeant's sweater. "Just a little while longer."

"Yes, but I..." Jun kept hold of her submachine gun with one hand, and with the other swiftly drew the Webley Mk VI from the holster at her hip and fired two rounds in short succession, taking out the two closest Dead to her current position.

"Wait for it!" the sergeant shouted back.

For a moment Jun was unsure what exactly she was meant to be waiting for. Then just as she was taking aim the Webley at another of the approaching Dead, she was surprised when its head exploded into a bloody mist before she'd even had the chance to pull the trigger.

Jun's gaze cut back the way they'd come, where she could see the light of the setting sun glinting off the lens of a rifle's scope atop one of the few standing walls in the ruined village, and heard the sound of another round being fired in the near distance. Werner, Curtis, and Sibyl must have gotten into position as the sergeant had ordered, and with the survivors having moved out of the field of fire, they were free to pick off the Dead at long range.

"Pull back!" the sergeant shouted as he fired another shotgun blast and took out another of the Dead that was trying to get around the downhill side. "The others'll cover our retreat!"

As the sergeant stepped in between Jun and the nearest of the oncoming Dead, she took the opportunity to yank out her Thompson's drum magazine and quickly swapped out the full one she pulled from her back. Then she in turn covered the sergeant's retreat with a few well-placed bursts of submachine gun fire into the oncoming horde, and the two of them continued to walk backwards down the road towards the village, as shots from their squad mates behind them picked off the forward most of the Dead one by one. But still the Dead came closer and closer.

Even with the number of undead bodies that they managed to put down, the oncoming tide of the bastards surged towards them. Thankfully none of the Dead were moving much faster than a shambling pace—not like some of the burning Dead that Jun had encountered from time to time, sprinting towards their enemies as flames consumed them whole, only to explode without warning—but they were relentless, inexorable, and they had the strength of numbers on their side.

Jun chanced a look back over her shoulder, and could see that the band of survivors had made it off the road, no doubt sheltering somewhere out of sight behind one of the village's ruined buildings. And now she could more clearly see Sibyl perched atop one of the walls, firing a round from her Lee Enfield at the advancing tide of Dead, and not far behind her was Curtis lining up a shot with his M1. Jun couldn't see Werner, but was sure he must be nearby.

So the immediate threat to the civilians was passed, and now Jun and the sergeant were the only ones under direct threat. But even with the rest of the squad covering their retreat, the two of them couldn't just break off and make a hasty retreat, not without running the risk that one of the Dead in the forefront might take the opportunity to lunge forward and attack while they were still in range. As it was, the quicker of the shambling Dead still managed to get almost within arm's reach before

Jun or the sergeant put them down with well-placed headshots; the Dead in the front of the vanguard were too close to the pair for the rest of the squad to snipe them from a distance without potentially hitting their teammates in the crossfire.

Perhaps a grenade might scatter the vanguard of the Dead enough to give us time to get clear, Jun thought. But a blast close enough to disrupt the nearest of the Dead would run the risk of hitting Jun and the sergeant as well. *If we'd had time to set up some sort of defensive explosive, then maybe…*

Before Jun could finish the thought, she heard a voice calling from behind them.

"Four more paces, sergeant, then you will want to step carefully."

Jun shot a glance back over her shoulder and saw that Werner was standing in the middle of the road a short distance downhill, taking aim with his Karabiner 98K bolt-action rifle and firing a round that whizzed just past her head and took out one of the Dead shambling towards her.

Werner worked the bolt to chamber another round, and then nodded in Jun's direction.

"Mind how you go, Fräulein," Werner said, and then pointed towards the ground in front of him. Jun could just make out a thin line like a spider's thread glinting a few inches above the road's surface and stretching from one side of the road to the other. "I will keep the verdammt Dead off of your backs."

Werner was backing away from the wire slowly as he fired another round past the sergeant, taking out another Dead that had been closing in.

"Okay, kid, you heard the man," the sergeant said, nodding in Jun's direction. "Get over and get to cover."

Jun was tempted to argue that with the Thompson she was in a stronger position to cover the sergeant's retreat than the other way around, but those were the orders she had been given and this was far from the appropriate time to debate the matter. She turned, quick-stepped until just short of the tripwire, and then gingerly stepped over the wire, first one foot carefully placed on the ground on the far side, then the other lifted up high and swung over with as much care as she could muster. When she was safely on the other side, she took two steps back and then shouted to the sergeant.

"I'm over, sir, now you go." Jun emptied what was left of the submachine gun's magazine in a spray across the entire oncoming vanguard from one side to the other as the sergeant turned, took three long strides, and then simply stepped over the tripwire like he was simply stepping over a crack in the sidewalk.

"Get going, y'all!" the sergeant shouted, and started sprinting down the road towards the village. Jun slung the Thompson over her shoulder and then she and Werner followed close on the sergeant's heels, pounding towards the ruins as quick as they could go.

Sniper fire from their squad mates atop the ruins kept the leading Dead from reaching the tripwire while Jun and the others were still in range. The forward-most of the Dead was now just a couple of shambling steps away from the tripwire, and there was nothing more than a few small boulders between Jun and the tripmines that she had glimpsed in the scant foliage on either side of the road. Knowing Werner, he would have placed the explosives where they would deliver the maximum results, and doubtless he would have ensured that the bulk of the blast was directed back uphill in the direction of the rest of the shambling horde. But still, Jun didn't want to be anywhere close by when the mines were tripped. Only a shambling step remained now, surely, as Jun poured on even more speed, breathless as she pushed herself to sprint even fast. But the Dead vanguard must have reached the tripwire by now? She risked a quick glance back over her shoulder and…

The fireball swelled like a flower blooming impossibly fast, the flash of light reaching Jun's eyes a fraction of a second before the deafening boom of the explosion reached her ears.

The Dead were engulfed in the flames, immediately set to burning like human torches. They did not go down all at once, though, but continued to shamble forwards, stumbling erratically and waving their limbs in a horrible dance as the fire consumed them. Rotten flesh and rancid muscle burned away to ash until they collapsed into greasy piles of blackened bones that continued to smolder and pop, all the while accompanied by inhuman howls and the sickening smell of burning flesh and hair.

A handful of Dead from the rear of the horde made it through the maelstrom with only minor burns, but sniper fire from Sibyl and Curtis dropped them long before they'd gotten close to the village.

It was some time before Jun was able to catch her breath, and even longer before she was willing to let her guard down and accept that the immediate danger had passed. And the smell of the burning Dead would linger in her nostrils for a long time to come.

CHAPTER 3

HOURS LATER, A partially burned Dead that had lost both legs and both arms up to the elbow dragged itself through the ash and fallen bodies of its former companions, inch by painful inch, until it had almost reached the entrance to the ruined village. But by that point the team had already set up a defensive perimeter, stringing up razor wire around an encampment with torches marking out each of the approaches. Jun had been busy digging a latrine when she spotted the near-limbless Dead dragging itself towards the camp. She almost had to admire the persistence of the damned thing. Almost. She removed the head from the torso with her shovel, not even bothering to draw her firearm, and then used the shovel to push the rotting remains a ways downwind from the camp before jogging back to rejoin the others.

"Any trouble out there, kid?" the sergeant asked

as Jun approached the campfire, wiping gore off the blade of her shovel as she drew near.

"Just a straggler," she answered, shaking her head and sliding the shovel back into her pack. "Nothing to worry about."

On the far side of the fire sat Werner, cleaning and oiling his rifle. Sibyl was heating up water in a valiant if ultimately doomed attempt to fix a pot of tea—her every attempt to brew up anything like a decent cup had resulted either in a scalding hot discolored water or lukewarm slurry that tasted of dirt, but still she kept trying—while Curtis was distributing emergency rations to the survivors who had fled down out of the mountains.

Satisfied with Jun's response, the sergeant turned his attention back to the survivors. Or rather, refugees, to be precise, since all of them had evidently covered considerable distances after fleeing from the Dead, only to find themselves driven together by geography and circumstances as they fled south out of the Alps.

There were eighteen of them in all, ten men and eight women, the youngest of them around Jun's age, and the oldest of them a grandmotherly type with a deeply-lined face and a nimbus of white hair around her head. How they related to one another Jun was not entirely sure, though it seemed that there were members of several different families among them, who clumped together in defensive knots as they huddled near the fire. They spoke a variety of languages, mostly Italian, German, and French, though Jun caught smatterings of English and what she thought might have been one of the Slavic tongues. And ever since the squad had finished setting up the camp as night fell, the sergeant had been trying to calm the refugees and to coax some sort of meaning out of the babble of frightened, weary voices.

"Why here?" one of the refugees was asking in broken English, clearly uncertain about the idea of remaining so close to the place where they had only narrowly escaped the pursuing Dead. He gestured behind them, away from the mountains and towards the south. "Go? Now?"

"Tomorrow, I promise," the sergeant answered in a calming tone, giving his most assuring smile. "It ain't safe to travel at night, so we'll hole up here, and when the sun's up my guys and I will get you down to our basecamp. They can help you get to the compound down south, where the rest of the survivors and refugees are staying 'till we get this mess cleaned up."

Jun wasn't sure how much of that the refugee had understood, but a number of small knots of conversations broke out, with questions whispered and answered in several languages, as the group attempted to translate for each other as best they could. Jun, who spoke Mandarin and Japanese as well as English and passable Russian, wished that Werner had volunteered to help translate, as his German would doubtless have come in handy. Sibyl only spoke English and a smattering of Tibetan, Hindi, and Arabic, while Curtis only spoke English, and neither the sergeant's English or the Creole French he'd grown up speaking were of much use at the moment. But Werner was not the best at interacting with civilians at the best of times, and the circumstances were far from ideal, so perhaps the sergeant was correct in declining to force the man to assist.

Even so, the sergeant was determined to piece together the story of how this unlikely group of refugees had come together, and just what had driven them across and down out of the Alps.

"Now, let's try this again and take it slow," he said. "Y'all can call me Josiah, and I'm in charge of this squad. My team and I are out here searching for survivors and cleaning up after past action, making sure that there aren't any pockets of the Dead left hiding here or there. But what you folks was running from…?" He shook his head, whistling low. "That wasn't any 'pocket' of the Dead. That was a whole damned chest o'drawers."

The refugees exchanged confused looks, and the sergeant hastened to clarify when they started asking him about clothing and furniture.

"Never mind about that," he said in a rush, holding up his hands to gesture for silence, "the point is that you folks were running away from a *much* bigger bunch of Dead bastards than we thought was still up and running around these parts. So my question to y'all is, where the hell did you run into the bastards in the first place?"

Jun could see the exhaustion on the faces of the refugees as they stared at the sergeant with a mixture of confusion and fear, and then broke into small knots of conversation as they translated his request into the various languages they spoke. Finally, one of the older members of the group, a grey haired man with an unshaven chin who looked to be about the age as Jun's mother, stood up, pointed to the north, and in deeply accented English simply said, "Mountain?"

The sergeant covered his eyes with his hand and sighed deeply. In response, the grey haired refugee turned to some of the other members of the group seated at the ground around him, and there was a rapid-fire exchange of questions and answers in

French before the spokesman turned back to the sergeant and clarified.

"Nazi. Dead. In mountain." One of the other refugees chimed in with a quick note, and the spokesman nodded quickly before adding, "Nazi Dead ON mountain."

The sergeant lowered his hands and fixed the spokesman with a hard stare.

"Look, old-timer," he said, sounding impatient, "we *saw* them chase you down out of the mountains, right? We get it. There were Dead Nazis roaming around up there. But how did all of y'all come to be running from 'em together? You didn't just go looking for trouble, I'm guessing."

A middle-aged woman dressed all in black with a scarf over her head made a rude gesture in the direction of the spokesman and then climbed to her feet, leaning heavily on a teenage boy seated beside her.

"Fortezza," she said, staring intently into the sergeant's face and looking for any sign of recognition. She motioned with her hands as if miming the outline of a box or building, and then pointed a bony finger towards the Alpine peaks to the north. "Si? Fortezza."

"Sergeant?" Jun chimed in as the sergeant scratched his chin and scowled. "It sounds as if she's saying…"

"Fortress? Right, I got that much," he answered. "But what the devil does that…?"

The sergeant was interrupted when Werner dramatically cleared his throat, signaling for attention. He and Jun turned to look over in his direction, where the German had finished reassembling his freshly cleaned and oiled Karabiner.

"You are correct, sergeant," Werner said, sounding at once bored and annoyed, "fortezza translates as stronghold or, yes, fortress."

Jun just blinked in Werner's direction.

"Hang on." The sergeant put his hands on his hips and tilted his head to one side, a quizzical expression on his face. "You speak Italian?"

Werner shrugged. "And a little French that I picked up in Normandy. But I had to learn Italian to coordinate with our allies in North Africa during the last war, when I served under Rommel."

The sergeant lowered his head, eyes closed, shoulders slumped with a weary sigh. "That's information that might have been useful a while back now, Werner."

Jun didn't bother pointing out that Werner could have just as easily translated for the one or two German speakers in the group. That he was conversational in both French and Italian meant that he could obviously communicate with almost any of the refugees, and had simply kept that information to himself before now.

"Would you mind?" The sergeant gestured towards the refugees while shooting a hard look in Werner's direction.

The German soldier just arched an eyebrow. It was almost as if he didn't have a clue what the sergeant was asking him to do and was genuinely confused. Jun was half-convinced that was an actual fact.

"Talk to these poor bastards and tell me what they're saying," the sergeant said through gritted teeth.

"Those are your orders?" Werner carefully set his rifle down on his pack, careful to keep its barrel up and out of the dirt.

The sergeant nodded, gritting his teeth even tighter. "Yes, I'm ordering you."

Werner stood up and dusted off his palms as he walked around the edge of the fire toward the spot where the refugees were gathered.

"As you wish," he said with a quick nod towards the sergeant.

Then he turned to address the refugees.

"Sprechen sie Deutsch?"

A few hands tentatively rose.

"Parlez-vous français?"

Werner nodded, noting a few more hands rising.

"Parla Italiano?"

Several more hands flashed in the air.

Werner turned his attention back to the sergeant. "Yes, I believe that I can translate for you. What is it you wish to know?"

The sergeant's shoulders shook with a ragged sigh of exasperation, his jaw tightening as he fought to maintain his composure. Jun didn't think that Werner was the type to intentionally antagonize a superior officer, but had he really been paying so little attention to the sergeant's abortive attempt to interrogate the refugees all of this time? Or was he just a stickler for the rules and for orders, and wouldn't dream of interviewing the refugees on his own recognizance when the sergeant had just specifically requested that Werner instead simply translate what the ragtag bunch was saying?

Jun thought that she detected the hint of a smile at the corner of Werner's mouth, and suspected that the answer might lie somewhere in the middle.

"Ask them," the sergeant began with exaggerated deliberateness, "under what circumstances"—he paused long enough for a deep breath, in and out—"they came into contact with such a large party of the enemy Dead, and where this happened. My fear is that there might be an even larger number of the bastards lurking around up there, and if so, the Resistance brass will want to know about it."

Werner stood to attention and replied with a short nod—and Jun thought that the man might have even clicked his heels together as he did, parade ground style—and then turned his attention fully to the refugees.

He began to question the group in sections, directing careful and deliberate inquiries in one language after another to the little pockets among them, sometimes following up with additional questions that appeared to be for clarification or additional context. Werner would nod meaningfully from time to time, and even appeared to be surprised on several occasions, a note of skeptical disbelief in his tone as he asked a follow up question. But there came a moment when he was stopped short all together, eyes widening and mouth hanging open a fraction as he stared at the group of refugees with an expression of slow-dawning alarm on his face, that slowly melted into a mask of fierce anger. He asked one final question in German of a pair of refugees, and when they nodded with assent he turned and took several steps away from the group, looking up at the

Alpine peaks which dominated the northern skies, eyes narrowed with determination as he stood still and silent as a statue.

"Well?" the sergeant finally said, gesturing broadly in Werner's direction.

"I will explain, but first…" Werner turned in the sergeant's direction, a deep frown lining his face. "I will need a stiff drink," he finished, in what seemed to Jun an uncharacteristically dark tone.

###

A SHORT WHILE later the five members of the deadhunter squad sat huddled close together near the edge of the razorwire fence. They were lit from above by a pair of brightly burning torches so that two sets of shadows fell on the ground before them: one from the left of the group and one from the right, shifting and skewing as the night's wind fanned the torches' flames and caused the shadows to flicker and dance across the hard-packed earth, like a pair of tiny armies battling to control contested ground.

"We thought it was a myth," Werner finally said, staring somewhere into the middle distance. "Himmler's last bit of propaganda to bolster the flagging confidence in the future of the Fatherland amongst the population in the final days of the war."

He paused and looked once more north towards the peaks of the Alps, which were now silhouettes standing against a star-spangled sky.

"Damn Hitler," Werner added in a low, vicious tone. "Damn him and the bootlicking toadies who stood beside him, damn them to hell."

"Well, now," Curtis put in, sounding a little skeptical, "you might well be a fountain of regret now that your side got us all in this mess, but weren't you the good little Nazi during the war?"

Werner bristled, and turned a dark gaze in the young American's direction.

"I was a loyal German soldier, and for my sins I allowed myself to believe the lies we were told about the Fatherland, and about our enemies. But I never had any faith in the Führer's cult of personality, and do not for a moment think to lump me in with those unprofessional zealots in the Waffen-SS." He paused for a moment, bringing his temper back under control. "I spent the last days of the war in a penal battalion after I put a bullet in the brain of an SS Ahnenerbe occultist I discovered committing an unholy occult rite in Carentan. My only regret was that I was arrested before I had a chance to put a bullet in the brain of Standartenführer Hermann Ziegler, the Waffen-SS colonel who had ordered him to perform the rite in the first place. As it was I would have ended up before a firing squad if not for Field Marshall Rommel, who felt that I could still be of some use to the war effort. As it was I was hard pressed to remain alive after months on end of suicide missions and operations against impossible odds. And all the while I had to endure endless talk from our SS overseers about their beloved Führer, and about his toady Himmler's plans to defeat the enemy no matter how long it took."

Werner's eyes once more darted towards the Alpine peaks to the north, and then looked back to Curtis before shifting his gaze to each of us in turn.

"Himmler planned to continue fighting the war," Werner continued, "even if Berlin fell. Even if Hitler himself were to die or be captured by enemy forces."

"And just precisely how did he intend to do that?" Sibyl cut in, an acid edge to her tone. It was clear that she had little faith that anything Werner was telling them was true, and even less patience for hearing him out. "Beyond raising the dead from beyond the grave to fight his war for him, of course."

Werner shook his head, a bitter expression on his face.

"This was long before any of us had heard

anything about Plan Z," he clarified. "Though to be honest, the idea of dead Nazis rising from their grave to wage war against the living would have seemed scarcely less difficult to credit that the notion of Himmler's supposed Alpine Redoubt."

"The Alpine what now?" the sergeant asked, sounding fairly skeptical himself.

Jun could see a flicker of recognition light in Curtis's face, though, and even Sibyl was beginning to display a begrudging level of trust.

"The last bastion for the Third Reich," Werner explained, "a fortress somewhere in the Alps. If German military command were to be defeated... If Berlin were to be overrun, and the Führer himself perhaps to fall... Then the party faithful and a handpicked army of Waffen-SS officers and Hitler Youth would make a strategic retreat to a fortified stronghold somewhere in the Alps with enough food and supplies to remain hidden for years on end, and enough arms and ammunition to continue waging war against their enemies for as long as the circumstances demanded."

"Is such a thing possible?" Jun found herself asking, unable to keep a tone of breathless disbelief out of her voice.

"As I say," Werner answered, "in the penal battalion we all thought it was a myth. Propaganda, intended to convince the German people to continue fighting long after hope would otherwise have been lost."

"It *was* a myth," Curtis cut in, "but it wasn't the German people they were trying to fool, but the Allies. Do you all have any idea how much time and energy the Americans wasted trying to *find* that Alpine Fortress after the invasion of Normandy? One of the other prisoners-of-war who were at Dresden with me had been on an expeditionary force that spent *ages* trudging all over those damned mountains looking for the blasted thing. The whole thing was intended to fool the Allies and send 'em off on a wild goose chase, to give the Nazi forces time to retreat and regroup."

Curtis shot an angry look at Werner, who only gave him a gentle smile and a nod in return.

"Fooling Germany's enemies would have been an added benefit, perhaps," Werner replied, "but I assure you, no one needed fooling more than the German people, who somehow still allowed themselves to believe that we had not become the villains of our own narrative, but were heroes who would clearly be victorious in the end. Who somehow clung to the delusion that God himself was on our side..."

A dark shadow fell across Werner's face and his jaw tightened, eyes narrowing to slits as his thoughts seemed to drift back to some unwanted recollection. He swallowed hard, and regained his composure.

"That's all well and good," the sergeant cut in, sounding a little impatient, "but what's all that got to do with the price of tea in China? Myth, propaganda, whatever you want to call it... what's that got to do with us in the here and now?"

Werner stood in silence for a moment before answering, his gaze travelling across the faces of his squad mates.

"If what these poor unfortunates tell me is correct," he finally replied, gesturing with a small wave of his hand at the refugees trying to rest on the far side of the camp fire, "then the Alpine Fortress is a reality, and the last war might not be as finished as we thought."

CHAPTER 4

JUN KNEW THAT she wasn't alone in having many questions about Werner Sauer's cryptic utterance about the Nazis' Alpine redoubt, but the discussion was suddenly sidetracked when an unholy and inhuman sound drifted in on the night breeze. It was a harsh, guttural susurration, a voice whispering urgently with its dying breath in some unknown and unearthly tongue. It was not the first time that Jun had heard such unsettling utterances. Far from it.

"We've got incoming," the sergeant said, jumping to his feet and retrieving his rifle and shotgun from where they had laid resting against his pack.

Large hordes like those that they had faced earlier in the day were rare occurrences for the deadhunter squad, and they had only encountered groups of similar number a few times before. More frequently encountered, however, were individual shamblers or small groupings of two, three, or four at a time: small bands that seemed to roam aimlessly across the landscape with no rhyme or reason, seeking only to devour the flesh of any living beings that they might chance to come across.

"Sibyl, you keep watch over the refugees," the sergeant said, checking the action on his Springfield rifle, "and shout out if you need backup. The rest of you, spread out to cover the approaches. I'll take high noon"—he swung one hand in a chopping motion towards the north side of the perimeter— "Curtis, you take three o'clock"—he pointed due east—"Werner, six o'clock"—he pointed towards the south—"and Jun, you take this side." And he nodded towards the nearest stretch of the razorwire enclosure, facing the western side of the village ruins.

Everyone retrieved their arms and ammunitions quickly and quietly, and broke off to their respective positions without needing any additional direction.

For the briefest moment, Jun was tempted to douse the torches which burned a handful of paces to either side of her. The light from them hindered her ability to see well or far in the dark, but would at the same time draw the Dead towards her position. If the Dead were driven by any instinct other than naked appetite it was a drive towards light and heat, so often associated with their living prey. A burning torch might serve to scorch the flesh of the Dead into ash, as Werner's tripwired explosive had done hours before, but a torch's light also drew the Dead into their orbit like moths to a flame.

Glancing back, she could see that Sibyl was in the process of dousing the camp fire, dumping a shovel-full of dirt over the burning logs and then stomping out the embers. Soon she and the refugees would be sitting in total darkness at the center of the defensive enclosure.

But would they remain hidden from the Dead? Jun wasn't sure. She had seen shambling corpses whose eyes were rotted out of their sockets who still seemed to be able to perceive where living bodies were in relation to itself. And surely the Dead weren't operating by a sense of smell, given how many of them were staggering around with noses rotted right off of their ruined faces. Did the Dead have some other sensory capabilities that the living lacked? They did seemed attracted to heat and light, after all. Or were they attracted by some sort of life essence itself?

Jun had heard many a late-night debate in the Woolwich barracks in London the past year while training with anti-necro specialists, and had even participated in a few heated discussions herself on occasion. Several of the more scientifically minded participants had been convinced that the Dead were somehow perceiving the infrared end of the electromagnetic radiation spectrum, and proposed ways in which this could be used to the Resistance's advantage, were it to be proven true. Others of a more spiritual bent insisted that the Dead were instead drawn by the souls of the living, and that it was some essence of spirit that the undead hungered for, rather than the literal flesh.

When the debates reached the point of outright hostility and arguments threatened to spill over into physical conflict was usually the point that Jun excused herself from the discussion and headed off to bed. But one thing was certain, whichever side of the debate had the correct answer. If she, a living being, were standing between two brightly lit torches, then she would serve as a kind of decoy, attracting the approaching Dead away from the terrified mass of refugees huddled in the darkness a farther distance away. Whether her own living spirit or essence, or the heat and light of the torches: either way she would draw the attention of the Dead away from the innocents she had sworn an oath to protect.

So Jun left the torches lit and kept her eyes narrowed as she scanned the outer darkness for movement, not failing to realize or admit that she allowed herself to follow such discursive paths of reasoning in part to keep herself from dwelling on any anxiety or fear that she might otherwise be experiencing because of the encroaching threat of the unknown. To keep from thinking too long or too hard about the fact that she was standing alone facing a darkness in which the unquiet Dead were abroad.

She took a deep breath and then expelled it slowly through her nostrils, conscious of the rhythm of her pulse thudding in her ears. *Trust the training*, she told herself. *Trust your instincts. Stay alive. You've been through this before.*

Her thoughts flashed on the image of her friends and colleagues being swallowed up by a tidal wave of relentless Dead in Moscow as she screamed her throat raw, helpless to do anything other than watch them die…

Jun shook her head, fiercely, as though she could shake loose those unwanted memories. She had already mourned her losses enough for one lifetime, and even if she had tears left to spill she would have to wait until she had the luxury to once again know grief. For now, there was a job to do.

She strained to listen, and there on the edge of hearing she once again heard that harsh inhuman whispering, unearthly and strange, seeming to echo back from all around her. It was impossible to tell just what direction the sound was coming from, but it was clearly growing closer.

"Anybody got eyes on it?" the sergeant called from the north edge of the enclosure, a dozen or so paces behind Jun and to her right.

"Nein," Werner sounded off, to Jun's left, answered by Curtis's simple "Nope" from behind her.

"I can hear them," Jun began, not taking her eyes off the darkness in front of her, "but so far I haven't seen…"

There. Right in front of her. The flickering light of the torch's flame was reflecting on something at eye level a short distance ahead of her, iridescent like light on spilled oil.

"Got something," Jun shouted, while raising her Thompson submachine gun to her shoulder and sighting on the spot where she'd seen the light reflected.

"Over here, too," Curtis called out from behind her.

Jun scarcely had time to blink when a rotting corpse shuffled into view, heading directly towards her. In the ruined face one eye still rested in its socket, although the pupil was cloudy and white, but the other eye had been knocked loose at some point, dangling at the edge of the dislodged optic nerve against a hollow cheek like a ball hanging at the end of a tether. But some kind of beetle seemed to have taken up residence in the empty socket, feasting on the decaying flesh, and it was the iridescent shell of the scarab-like insect that Jun had seen the light reflecting against.

Another shuffling step towards her, the Dead's mouth working unsettlingly back and forth as that inhuman guttural whisper ushered forth from somewhere deep within.

Jun could hear Curtis firing repeatedly behind her, shouting obscenities as he did. She didn't bother with boasts or war cries herself, but simply squeezed the trigger of the submachine gun and drove a bullet through the Dead's skull right through the milky white eye.

As the Dead collapsed to the ground, the beetle unfolded its wings and jumped away, startled.

"Contact," Werner called from Jun's left, and his MP40 barked in his hands as he fired into the darkness.

Jun watched the tiny beetle perched on the ground beside the decaying corpse for a brief instant. Then the insect unfolded its wings again and took flight.

"Damn," she heard the sergeant saying from her right, "I've got one of the bastards on this side, too."

As the sergeant's 12-gauge shotgun made short work of the approaching Dead, Jun's attention stayed with the beetle. For a moment she worried that it might fly too close to the torch's flame, but it rose up and out of the sphere of torchlight and into the night sky above, unscathed and unsinged.

The Dead were her enemy, and she had made a sacred promise to protect the living. She found some comfort in the fact that she had not been forced to harm a living creature to bring down one of the undead enemy, even a creature as small and seemingly insignificant as a beetle.

"All quiet?" the sergeant called out after a long silence. "Sound off, y'all."

"No movement east," Curtis answered.

"South is clear," Werner added.

"And to the west?" the sergeant called over after a moment. "Kiddo, where are we at?"

Jun blinked, realizing that she had gotten caught up in the reverie of watching the beetle disappear into the darkness. She trained her attention back on the darkness before her, straining with each of her senses.

"Nothing," she finally replied. "One hostile

approached, but it's down."

"Seems like they came at us from all four sides," the sergeant said, stepping back from the razorwire and lowering his shotgun.

"Almost like a coordinated attack, *nicht wahr*?" Werner observed from the other side of the enclosure.

"But they're not supposed to be able to do that, are they?" Curtis sounded equal parts skeptical and alarmed.

"If I might," Sibyl chimed in from the center of the encampment, "isn't it equally likely simply to be a coincidence, and that four lone shamblers were drawn by the heat and light of our campfire and torches at the same time?"

"But the four of them all *arriving* at the same time, too?" The sergeant turned away from the razorwire, and from the light of the flickering torches Jun could see the look of uneasy disbelief on his face. "That's a mighty big coincidence, you ask me."

"But what, I ask, is the alternative?" Sibyl went on, while setting about the business of relighting the main campfire. "A heretofore unknown level of communication and coordination amongst the mindless undead?"

"Perhaps that is exactly the solution, Frau Beaton." Werner approached the center of the enclosure, slinging his MP40 over his shoulder. "It would be in line with much of what our friends here have told me." He nodded curtly towards the huddled refugees.

Jun was curious to ask Werner just what he meant by that, but the sergeant forestalled any further discussion.

"There'll be time enough to continue this conversation tomorrow on our way down to base camp," he said, his tone making it clear that he was not inviting debate on the matter. "We best get what rest we can in the meantime. We'll take it in shifts to cover the approaches, and anyone not on sentry duty best get what sleep they can. Jun and Curtis, you've got first shift. Wake me and Sibyl in a couple of hours, and then she can catch a little more shuteye while Werner and I cover the last shift before dawn."

As the others settled themselves down to sleep around the restoked campfire, Jun busied herself reloading a fresh magazine drum for her Thompson, and then started to walk the interior perimeter of the enclosure. Curtis was still in position on the eastern edge of the razorwire, and didn't seem to be planning on moving any time soon.

In response to a sharp glance from Jun, he just shrugged.

"My ears work just as well standing still as walking around, you know," he said. "Hey, you wouldn't happen to have any smokes on you, would you?"

It was not the first time the American had tried to cadge cigarettes off of her, and she was sure it would not be the last. But she couldn't fault him for trying, as annoying as it was.

"Again, I do not smoke," she said as she walked past him.

"Well, I do," he said, and pulled a half-full pack out of his breast pocket. He shook one out, stuck it in the corner of his mouth, and then lit it with the flame of the nearest torch.

"If you had cigarettes, why try to get one from me?" Jun said, pausing for a moment to look back in his direction with a perplexed expression on her face.

"Why smoke mine if I could smoke yours instead?" Curtis answered with a lopsided grin.

Jun just shook her head, and continued on her rounds, listening for the sounds of more Dead out in the darkness. The image of her friends in Moscow once more flashed into her mind but she pushed it from her, and instead concentrated on the memory of that tiny life that she'd seen fly up into the night sky, rising up above all of the terror and misery on the ground below.

CHAPTER 5

JUN WOKE SHORTLY before dawn, as the skies in the east were just beginning to lighten, the sun still hidden somewhere over the horizon. The little sleep she'd had in the night had been fitful and short, plagued by the usual nightmares. As always, she had dreamt about being out on patrol with the deadhunter squad, encountering the enemy, and finding herself overwhelmed by the onrushing hordes of the undead before finally jolting awake, heart racing and breathing hard. And as always, it took her a brief instant to realize that she was not about to be consumed by an undead fiend, and that she and her squad had survived the previous day and night unscathed.

In essence, Jun's nightmares were identical to her waking hours, up to a point. It was maintaining the difference between the two—ensuring that she was the one who prevailed, and not the enemy

Dead—that kept Jun on her toes.

As she rose, stretching her protesting muscles and rubbing a sore spot on her lower back, Jun checked the time on her wrist watch. It was already full daylight back home in Datong, and as always found herself wondering what the surviving members of her family were doing with their day. Her mother was probably still at the market procuring the ingredients for the evening meal, most likely, and Jun's younger brothers would still be at their daily studies. She had not seen any of them since she had left home to accompany the diplomatic mission to Moscow, and she sometimes wondered whether she ever would again.

"All right, y'all," the sergeant called out as he kicked dirt over the dying embers of the campfire. "Up and at 'em, we've got a lot of ground to cover today."

Curtis was still snoring, curled up in a ball on the hard dirt a short distance from where Jun now stood. She walked over and nudged his foot with the tip of her own boot. "Wake up!"

"Knock it off, will ya?" Curtis moaned without bothering to open his eyes. He waved one hand in a feeble gesture, as if plagued by a fly that he couldn't quite muster the energy to shoo away.

"Sergeant says it's time to get moving," Jun said,

nudging his foot a little harder. Then she grinned, and leaned over him with her hands on her hips. "Wait too long and he just might pour ditch water over you again…"

That got the American up and moving. The sergeant had only pulled that prank once before, a few weeks previous, but apparently being awakened suddenly by getting doused in near-freezing muddy water was enough to make an impression.

"All right, all right," he said, pushing himself up into a sitting position and prying open one eyelid. "That's the last thing I need."

Jun hid a smile behind her hand as Curtis climbed to his feet, grumbling and swearing beneath his breath.

"There a problem over there?" the sergeant called over from the far side of the camp, where he was helping Sibyl distribute emergency rations to the refugees.

"Nah, everything's fine, sarge," Curtis replied with a weary wave, and then began lacing up his boots.

The sergeant caught Jun's eye and gave her a broad wink before turning his attention back to the refugees.

"What I'll never understand," Jun said as she

busied herself rolling up her own bedroll, "is how you sleep so soundly on the ground in the first place."

Curtis shrugged and he shoved his supplies back into his backpack. "Sister, the things I've slept through before now, like back in Dresden? If I'm not having to worry about the roof collapsing on my head or...?" He paused, shaking his head ruefully. "I'll take sleeping in the dirt any day of the week, if it means not having to worry about the sky falling down on top of me."

By the time Jun straightened up, her backpack settled on her back, her rifle slung over one shoulder and her submachine gun over the other, Werner had finished extinguishing the torches that had burned through the night and was in the process of lashing them together in one bundle. One of the torches slipped free as he was tying them together, though, and fell to the ground with a clatter. Werner almost lost his grip on the rest of the bundle, and in his successful attempt to keep it from collapsing was prevented from stopping the errant torch from rolling across the ground and out of his reach.

The escaping torch came to a stop a short distance from the spot where Sibyl was packing up her own supplies.

"Frau Beaton...?" Werner was struggling to keep the armload of torches from slipping out of his grasp, and looked to the Englishwoman with a pitiable expression on his face. Jun couldn't help but note the contrast between the cold efficiency that the German veteran displayed when engaged in combat operations, and his comparative lack of experience and confidence when dealing with more mundane tasks. "If you wouldn't mind?"

"I couldn't possibly," Sibyl responded without turning around, tightening the shoulder straps on her backpack. "I've far too many things to see to, myself."

The Englishwoman was already walking away, leaving Werner perched in an awkward position with his legs splayed wide to either side, his arms wrapped tightly around the bundle of torches.

Jun hurried over and picked up the errant torch in one hand, and then carried it back to where Werner was standing.

"Many thanks, Fraulein," Werner said as he opened his arms just wide enough for Jun to slip the torch back in amongst the others in the bundle. Then Jun held the torches in place while he finished lashing the bundle together.

"I don't think that it is you personally whom she dislikes," Jun said, glancing in the direction that Sibyl had gone. "I just think that perhaps she blames your entire country for the death of her husband."

Werner shrugged as he hoisted the bundle of torches onto his shoulder.

"I do not need her to like me," he said, slinging his Karabiner onto his shoulder. "Nor come to my assistance in such trivial matters. So long as Frau Beaton has my back when we are facing the verdammt Dead, I will be content."

As Werner began to walk away, he paused for a moment, a thoughtful expression on his face.

"Of course, it is possible that I was the one who killed her husband," he said, as though mulling over an odd bit of trivia that had just occurred to him. "I killed a great many soldiers in North Africa, and I imagine that many of them left widows behind. Frau Beaton might well be one of them."

With that the German soldier turned and walked in the direction of the sergeant, who was organizing the refugees into marching order.

Jun stared after Werner for a moment, blinking in silence. There was nothing prideful or boasting about his statement, but neither was there anything like regret. It was more like an athlete reflecting on scores won against members of the opposing team after a match, without any particular malice against or sympathy for those whom he had defeated. Not that war appeared to be a game to the German, far from it. One usually found some measure of happiness in sport, and found joy in winning a game; but Werner did not appear to find his victories in wartime as a source of any sort of happiness or joy. His manner was more that of a workman who took pride in his day's labor, but would just as soon have spent his time doing something else if the circumstances had been different.

###

JUN HAD WANTED to ask Werner to elaborate on what he had been saying the night before about the Nazis' alpine fortress before they had been interrupted by the encroaching Dead, but the awkward tension with Sibyl had distracted her, and now the squad was preparing to move out. Jun thought she might have a chance to give voice to her questions once the sergeant had given them their marching orders, but another burgeoning conflict involving Sibyl distracted her once again.

The group was moving south along the main road, with the sergeant in the lead, the bulk of the refugees following behind with Sibyl and Curtis flanking them on either side, and Jun and Werner bringing up the rear. The sergeant was addressing the company, deadhunter squad and refugees alike, as they moved.

"We've got a long day's hike ahead of us, y'all," he was explaining, "but Lord willing and the creek don't rise we'll get to our base camp before sunset."

Some of the refugees exchanged uneasy glances, and Jun could make out snippets of conversations about waterways in their path and the possibility of flooding.

"I just mean we'll be there barring catastrophe, is all," the sergeant clarified, sounding a little exasperated. "Just a bit of luck and we'll be fine."

Jun had been confused by the sergeant's idioms herself on more than one occasion, so she could hardly blame the refugees for being perplexed by his sometimes circuitous turns-of-phrase.

As she waited for an opportune moment to ask Werner to expand on what he had been saying about Himmler's strategic retreat, Jun scanned the horizon, wary and watchful for any sign of the Dead.

"Don't worry about shamblers roaming at long range," the sergeant called back from the head of the line, almost as if he had sensed her concern.

"Our first priority is to get these civilians to cover. Anyway, we crossed that last village off our map so we're due for a debrief and a bit of R&R as it is. If any Dead bastards come close, put 'em down, but otherwise we'll leave any scattered roamers out there for the next squad to handle."

That was well enough for Jun. She was about to ask Werner about what the refugees had told him the day before, and his comment about the Dead coordinating or communicating amongst themselves, when her attention was drawn by a loud exchange between Sibyl and Curtis.

"Hey, Sibyl, did I ever tell you about Joe Thompson, Jim Tierny, and Jonathan Taylor?" Curtis was saying, calling out over the heads of the refugees shuffling along between them. "Three guys I was in Basic with, who all had the same initials, first middle and last. Two of 'em even had the same birthdate. When it turned out that all three of them had dated women named Sally you'd have thought they'd unlocked the secrets of the pyramids, the way the three of them carried on about it. Had to mean something, right? It was written in the stars or some sort of malarkey like that. They were brothers in arms, destined to fight alongside each other to the bitter end. Only then they found out that they'd all three dated the *same* woman named Sally, who clearly had a particular type that she preferred, and all three of them ended up in the brig for disorderly conduct after a three-way boxing match broke out in the barracks. Two of them celebrated their shared birthday behind bars, while the third just mourned the loss of the teeth that had gotten knocked out of his grin in the course of the fight."

Sibyl fixed him with a haughty stare, leaning to one side to look past the backs of the refugees walking between them. "My dear boy, what*ever* are you babbling about?"

"The point is, I've seen stranger coincidences than a few shamblers coming out of the woodwork at the same time, lady."

Sibyl sighed dramatically.

"Of course," Curtis went on before she had a chance to reply, "all three of the poor bastards died on the same day during the Battle of the Bulge, so maybe they had some kind of shared destiny, after all. So it goes."

"Granted," Sibyl shot back in a rush, as if worried that the young American would carry on talking if she didn't speak up first, "given a long enough time span one will doubtless encounter any number of unlikely confluence of events. That simply stands to reason, given the nature of randomness and a sufficiently large sample size. But there are limits to what reason will bear, clearly, and the mere fact that coincidental relationships between acausal events exist doesn't by extension prove that all a-causal connections must be coincidental."

Now it was Curtis's turn to treat her to a blank stare.

"It's like my Chester always used to say," she went on, "the absence of evidence is not the evidence of absence."

"Lady," Curtis said with a snorting laugh, "what the heck are *you* babbling about?"

Sibyl shook her head sadly, like a teacher disappointed with a student who had done poorly on an exam because he'd failed to study and prepare properly. "Simply that there is a threshold beyond which a congruence of unlikely connections cannot simply be dismissed as coincidence, and the only rational course is to consider whether there might be some greater meaning, or some larger force at work."

"What, like the devil made 'em do it?" Curtis chuckled. "Because if so, I've gotta say that I'm kind of flattered. I wouldn't have bet that we'd be worth the attention."

"I'm not talking about any particular dogma or doctrine," Sibyl shot back, "simply that there is meaning to existence that sometime reveals itself in unexpected ways and…"

"Enough already, y'all," the sergeant called back from the head of the line, sounding annoyed. "Less talking, and more walking."

"But sergeant," Jun began to protest, not yet having found the opportunity to steer the conversation back to the more pressing questions surrounding the stories of the Alpine Redoubt. She did not dispute the fact that the idea of potential coordination or even direction amongst the movements of the Dead was worth discussing, but not when it so quickly devolved into one of Sibyl and Curtis's customary debates about nihilism, meaning, and humanity's place in an uncaring world—variations of which Jun had heard countless times in the months that she had been serving with the Englishman and the young American. "What about…?"

"No buts, kid," the sergeant shot back with note of finality to his voice. "Keep your eyes peeled for any Dead bastards, and keep chatter to a bare minimum."

And so Jun fell in line as the squad and the refugees under their protection continued to march south along the main road, as the sun rose slowly in the slate grey skies above.

CHAPTER 6

Jun and the rest of the squad were used to long marches through varying terrain and unreliable weather, but the refugees were civilians whose reserves had already doubtless been sorely tested by their long and stressful flight down out of the mountains. And while none of the refugees had complained about fatigue or hunger, clearly eager to put as much distance between themselves and any Dead who might still be pursuing them from the north, it was clear that the journey was beginning to take its toll.

So in the early afternoon, not too long after the sun had crested its zenith and begun sinking once more towards the western horizon, the sergeant called the column to a halt and ordered a thirty-minute-long rest. They would not be stopping long enough to set up a defensive perimeter, but instead he had the squad positioned on a low rise above the defile where he had asked the refugees to shelter, from which vantage Jun and the others could see the approaches from all four sides.

As the refugees passed around canteens and snacked on emergency supplies, the squad rested in the shade of a looming cypress tree, their weapons close at hand.

"Now, Werner, about this Alpine Fortress?" the sergeant said, finally returning to the topic that had been biting at Jun's curiosity since the night before. "You said that maybe the last war wasn't as finished as we thought?

Judging from the expressions on the faces of Sibyl and Curtis, it was clear that they shared Jun's burning interest as the three of them turned their attention from the sergeant to the German soldier sitting across from him.

"And that there was something in the refugees' account of what they'd experienced that suggested a level of coordination among the Dead?" the sergeant added. "Care to explain what you meant by that?"

Werner was eating potted meat from a tin, and finished chewing before answering, holding up one finger to signal for a moment's pause. Then he wiped his mouth with the back of his hand, took a long swig from his canteen, and then turned to meet the collective gaze of his four squad mates.

"Because that is what these poor unfortunates told me," he said simply, nodding in the direction of the refugees sitting huddled in the low depression that stretched behind the rise where the squad was perched. "They come from all over the Alps, as you might well have guessed from the welter of languages and accents in which they speak. Many of them fled south into the mountains from the foothills in Switzerland and France in the weeks and months following the rise of the Dead, seeking to find some refuge in the higher elevations. But there they encountered families of survivors fleeing *down* from the mountains to the east."

He paused, and pointed out a small knot of refugees sitting slightly apart from the others, looking a little more haggard and world-weary than the rest.

"These were residents in a remote Alpine village high in the Swiss Alps. They came with stories of seeing the German army moving large convoys into the mountains beginning in the winter of 1944. A small army of Waffen-SS officers and Hitler Youth led by an SS colonel, escorting dozens upon dozens of trucks. Engineers constructed what sounds like a sort of makeshift funicular railroad, with cables and tracks ferrying carts heavily laden with crates of ammunition, weapons and food up the side of the highest peaks themselves, to some kind of base that was kept carefully hidden from the view of anyone below. Then the funicular railroad was disassembled after it had carried the SS officers and Hitler Youth up to the peak, like a man pulling a rope ladder up after himself after reaching his destination, and the trucks were driven back down out of the mountains and never seen again. The villagers kept careful watch to see whether any of the officers or their young charges ever came back down the mountain again, but none of them were ever seen again."

Werner paused, his jaw tightening.

"Until the day that Plan Z was enacted," he added, "and the villagers saw the first of the Dead who came down off of the mountaintops and attacked the village."

Jun glanced around the circle at the other members of the squad, and saw that they were as intrigued and confused as she herself felt. A small army ascending a mountain to wait out the end of the fall of the military command? That was not too difficult to believe. And they all knew too well how it had gone the day that the enemy dead had risen from their graves, animated by some unholy rites carried out by Hitler and his lackeys in the

Ahnenerbe, the Nazis' occult society. But was there some connection between the two?

"You said something about coordination or even control," the sergeant responded.

Werner nodded, taking another long swig of water from his canteen. If Jun didn't know better, she would be tempted to think that the canteen actually held stronger spirits instead, schnapps or brandy, the way that the German soldier seemed eager to use it to settle his uneasy nerves.

"The people of the village were convinced that the Nazis on the mountaintop were sending the Dead out into the world to do their bidding. Understand, they were more or less completely cut off from the lowlands by this point, and when the undead first approached them from the direction that they had seen the Waffen-SS officers and the Hitler Youth ascending, the connection seemed obvious to them. But even after they encountered refugees fleeing upland and away from the low country that the Dead were already overrunning, the villagers continued to insist that the undead who plagued them were being directed in some way by the Nazis from on high. And the lowland refugees who had joined them as they fled together south and west through the Alps? They came to share the villagers' views."

Werner glanced again at the refugees seated below, and Jun could see a look of sympathy and perhaps even pity flickering across his face before he turned back to the squad to continue. And was that something like guilt that Jun could see twisting Werner's mouth into a frown? Considering how even-handedly he'd talked about making widows of so many woman like Sibyl during the campaigns in North Africa, evidencing no sign of guilt for the lives he'd taken on the battlefield, was it possible that he might be taking some personal responsibility for whatever hardships had befallen the refugees? Men, women, and children whom he'd never met before the day before, fleeing from undead horrors of precisely the sort that Werner had dedicated himself to eradicating as a member of a Resistance deadhunter squad. Jun wasn't sure, but it certainly looked to her as if Werner seemed to be taking the refugees' circumstances personally in a way that she couldn't quite put her finger on.

Perhaps that was why Werner had not spoken again about the Alpine Fortress through the hours of the night and the first half of the day, until prompted to do so once more by the sergeant when they finally paused for a break? Was he somehow reluctant to explain what his earlier cryptic statements had meant?

"The refugees were not simply fleeing from the Dead," Werner continued after a long pause, "they were being *pursued* by the Dead. Do you see the difference? We have all of us encountered countless shambling obscenities in the course of our duties, and I am certain you would agree that they are little more than unholy appetite given form and movement. The Dead hunger after the flesh or souls, or whatever you will, of the living, and it is this that drives them, but there is no true agency in their actions. Put another living body in between yourself and a Dead who is advancing on you, and the Dead will go after the nearer and easier of the prey one hundred percent of the time. But the horde of Dead which came down off of that mountain and attacked the villagers? They continued to pursue the villagers who survived long enough to flee, up and over the mountain passes and down south through the foothills, long past the point where any other undead that we have encountered would have broken off in favor of easier prey."

"Maybe the pickings up there were just slim," the sergeant put in, the first of the squad to interrupt Werner's account in several long moments. Jun realized that it was the longest unbroken speech that she had heard from the German soldier since they had first started serving together, months before. "They kept on pursuing the refugees from the village because there wasn't any other dining options on the go up there."

Werner shook his head.

"The refugees say that at one point a large herd of Alpine ibex crossed their path—mountain goats, outnumbering the refugees by nearly two to one. The refugees were sure that this would prove to be their salvation, if they could keep the herd between themselves and the pursuing Dead. Surely the Dead would be drawn to the burning life force or the ibex, or their lifeblood, or heat and warmth or whatever else it is that they crave from the living. But no. The Dead scarcely noticed the mountain goats, but waded right through the herd, batting them aside as they continued in their pursuit of the refugees without deviation or pause."

"Do the Dead even *eat* goats?" Curtis saw the sharp look that Sibyl was shooting in his direction, and he added, "I mean, have *you* ever seen one of those walking maggot factories eating a goat, lady?"

Sibyl crossed her arms over her chest, her nose in the air.

"Maybe it's a species thing," Curtis went on. "If a goat were to come back as one of the undead, would it hunger after the flesh of living *goats* instead of humans?"

"I'm fairly certain that ibexes are herbivores," Sibyl said without making eye contact with him, as though reluctant to engage on the American's level but unable to prevent herself correcting what she perceived as a flaw in his reasoning.

"We all saw those undead bastards tear their way through a whole damn herd of cattle in an afternoon at that ranch in Lombardy last month," the sergeant replied, "so I'm pretty sure a Dead bastard with an appetite ain't about to draw the line at mountain goat."

"When have you ever seen one of the Dead *without* an appetite?" Jun chimed in, but quickly turned her attention back to Werner, who had remained silent through the exchange. "So the refugees believe that the Dead had been sent down out of the Nazis' secret base in the mountain top to attack them personally?"

Werner had a far off look in his eyes for a moment, then turned and met Jun's gaze and nodded slowly.

"Do they say why?" Jun asked. "Why is that they think that the Nazis wish to see them dead... these villagers in particular, I mean, as well as the other refugees who have fallen in with them?"

"They believe that it is because they know

the rough location of the Alpine Redoubt," he explained in a low voice, as though worried that the refugees might overhear him. Or perhaps as if worried that someone else would, instead. "They believe that Nazis are conducting their war upon the living from their place of hiding high atop the Alps, and are using the Dead to eliminate anyone who might know the way to reach their secret fortress."

"That doesn't make a lick of sense," Curtis spat. "If they were covering their tracks why wouldn't the goose-stepping bastards have murdered the villagers on their way *up* the mountain in the first place?"

"The villagers say that while everyone in the region had observed the Nazis moving equipment up the mountain over the course of that winter, only a handful of people living the village had observed the bulk of the Nazi army ascending the mountain on that final day—a group of young villagers who had been out skiing, a hunter returning home, and a game warden on his rounds," Werner replied. "They had seen the face of the Waffen-SS colonel who led the final complement of men and boys up the mountainside, but they had kept themselves hidden from the colonel's view, worried to draw his attention lest they invite reprisals. But after the makeshift cable car had been dismantled and the trucks had returned to the lowlands, the villagers were much more open, sharing gossip in the village square about what they had seen, until it was not just the few young skiers, the hunter, and the game warden who knew the identity of the colonel who commanded the secret mountaintop army, but the entire village."

Werner took a deep breath and let out a ragged sigh.

"The villagers believe that they cursed themselves when they first spoke the SS colonel's name out loud," he went on. "That they invited doom on themselves and their families in that moment, ensured that the unholy forces of the Nazis would pursue them tirelessly until the ends of the Earth until the last person who knew about the secret Nazi fortress was eliminated."

"Sounds like a bunch of hooey to me," Curtis said with a sneer.

"I must admit, it does sound unlikely," Sibyl put in, making eye contact with Werner for the briefest of instants before averting her gaze once more.

"Nothing I've seen since this whole damned mess started makes me think that anything like that could be going on," the sergeant said, shaking his head slowly. "The Dead get up, they walk around eating whatever they get their hands on and making a powerful mess, and then we come along and put the bastards back in the ground. Ain't no grand plans or hidden agendas to it, just the living versus the Dead, that's all."

But Jun had spotted something in Werner's explanation, and seen a pained expression flit across his face once or twice as he had been talking. There was something more that he wasn't saying. Some vital bit of the story that connected to him personally, in ways that he found painful to consider.

She thought that she might know what it was.

"Who is he?" Jun asked, staring hard at Werner's face. "The Nazi colonel who led the secret army up the mountain, the one whose name said aloud brought doom on the village?"

Werner's gaze was on the ground at his feet, and he did not move or speak for long moments after Jun had asked her question.

Jun looked up and saw the sergeant and the others exchanging glances with raised eyebrows and shrugs. None of them saw quite where Jun was heading with this line of questioning, but she didn't think this was the time to explain. Better to wait and see if her suspicions were borne out.

Then Werner slowly lifted his head, and when

his eyes met Jun's she could see that the suspicions she had harbored had been correct.

"I was sent to a penal battalion after I shot and killed a member of the SS Ahnenerbe who was carrying out an unholy occult ritual in Carentan. I could not conscience that such a foul creature would be allowed to breath the same air as I, much less serve beneath my country's flag at my side. I was arrested on the spot, under the orders of that occultist's superior officer, who was the ranking member of the Waffen-SS on the site. Had I reacted more quickly, I could have put a bullet into *his* brain as well, and sent him to hell along with the occultist who I had just sent there. Had I been more strategic in my thinking, I would have shot the officer first, since the poor unfortunates who had died on that sacrificial altar were already dying by the time I killed the occultist, and so my bullet would not have brought them back from the brink. Had I shot the officer first, though, perhaps it might have forestalled future deaths. But no, I acted in the heat of the moment and shot the occultist, and the officer who had ordered the ritual in the first place lived to commit still further atrocities while I fought to survive in a penal battalion on the front lines."

Werner took a deep breath and blinked slowly.

"That officer was Standartenführer Hermann Ziegler, a colonel in the Waffen-SS." He paused, and glanced one last time at the refugees huddled down in the defile. "And it was the same Standartenführer Ziegler who the villagers saw leading the army up to the hidden fortress on the mountaintop."

Werner closed his eyes, seeming to retreat within himself for a moment before turning back to the squad and finishing his tale.

"The Nazi officer who I should have killed when I had the chance is in command of the secret army in the hidden Alpine Fortress, and if the villagers' suspicions are correct, he possesses some unknown power to control the Dead and force them to do his bidding."

The rest of the squad exchanged uneasy glances.

"Or maybe," Curtis said out of the corner of his mouth, "and I'm just talking hypothetically here you understand, maybe the villagers are talking out of their hats and the whole thing is just a coincidence?"

Werner turned and fixed the young American with a hard stare.

"Is that a gamble you are willing to take?" Werner said, eyes narrowed and jaw set. "Are you willing to stake your life on that certainty?"

Curtis opened his mouth to answer, but then closed it again, and instead sat in uncomfortable silence while he reconsidered his response.

"Okay, let's get this train rolling again, y'all," the sergeant said, pushing himself up onto his feet and picking up his rifle. Then he turned to look back over his shoulder at the German shoulder. "You sure about all of that, Werner?"

"In truth? No, I harbor doubts." Werner shouldered his own Karabiner. "These poor unfortunates have known nothing but terror and uncertainty since their ordeal began, and I don't know that they have the most objective view of their circumstance. Our young American friend might well be right, and this could all be superstition and coincidence. But I also fear that ignoring the possibility that it *is* true would be too great a risk to take."

CHAPTER 7

WITH ONLY A couple of hours left until sunset, and about that long to go until they reached basecamp, Curtis tempted fate.

"Pretty countryside," he said, glancing around at the surrounding countryside, placid and serene. "Quiet, too. Guess we've seen the last of the Dead for one mission…"

And at that moment, a skeleton burst out of the ground directly in his path.

"Dammit!" Curtis spat, fumbling to unsling his Slyskawica submachine gun from his shoulder as he took several staggering steps backwards.

"The devil…?" the sergeant began, glancing back over his shoulder upon hearing the commotion. His eyes widened as he saw the skeleton lurching towards the young American, and he swung up the barrel of his 12-gauge shotgun. "Incoming!"

Jun, Werner, and Sibyl reacted immediately,

moving into defensive positions around the refugees who huddled fearfully together in the middle of the road.

The sergeant's shotgun fired with a deafening blast, knocking off the top third of the undead fiend's skull, but still the skeleton lurched forward, bony hands out and grasping towards Curtis.

"Dammit!" Curtis spat once more, and raised his own submachine gun to fire.

Jun watched as a rapid-fire burst from Curtis's Slyskawica blew off bits of bone and gristle from the animated skeleton, but still it advanced. She could see the burning heart of the fiend shining from within the rotting ribcage, pulsing with unholy life and energy.

She raised her rifle to her shoulder and peered through the sight, training her fire on the glow of the heart within the chest. With the skeleton only one shambling step away from reaching Curtis, she squeezed off a round, hitting the fiend dead-center in its burning heart.

With a thrumming boom and an outrushing of air like a sudden wind gust, the skeleton's heart exploded into flames, reducing the fiend's bones to an expanding cloud of splinters that shot outwards in every direction.

"Good shot, kid. Got so caught up in the moment

that I forgot my own training for a moment." There was an undercurrent of tension to the sergeant's voice. He turned to the others as he worked his shotgun's pump and chambered another round. "Remember, y'all. Headshots for your garden-variety shamblers, but for these damned skeletons you want to direct your fire at the glowing heart in the chest."

Sibyl and Werner nodded in unison, though Jun was sure that neither of them realized it, while Curtis's own response was a little more frenetic.

"Where the hell did that thing come from?!" he shouted.

"From beneath the ground it would appear, dear boy," Sibyl replied casually.

Curtis rolled his eyes and sighed dramatically. "Well, *obviously*, but what the heck is an undead Nazi skeleton doing in the ground here to begin with?"

Jun and Werner were both scanning the road at their feet and the surrounding countryside, watchful for any further sign of subterranean Dead.

"Come on, now, Curtis," the sergeant said in a slightly scolding tone. "We've all run into these bony bastards from time to time. No need to get wrapped around the axle about it now."

"But sarge," Curtis shot back, pointing with the barrel of his submachine gun at the divot in the ground from where the skeleton had erupted only moments before. "It's like it was just lying there, waiting for us."

"Maybe it was just waiting for *anyone*," Jun called over, her eyes still roaming the ground all around them. "This is the main road into the basecamp from the north, after all. Any number of squads on patrol would pass this way when heading back in from making inspection tours."

The sergeant nodded, rubbing his lower lip with the tip of his index finger, thoughtfully. "Could be," he finally said, "could be, kiddo."

"But were that the case," Sibyl said, "it would stand to reason that there would be more than one meager skeleton lying in wait then, surely?"

Werner cleared his throat, a short guttural sound, drawing the squad's attention. When Jun and the others glanced in his direction, he simply nodded towards the south.

"You may be more right than you realize, Frau Beaton," Werner said, the stock of his Karabiner at his shoulder, his eye peering through the sight, finger poised over the trigger.

Even without the aid of a telescopic lens Jun could see exactly what Werner was referring to. A cloud of dust was billowing up into the air directly south of their present position, stretching in a wide arc from one side of the roadway to the other.

"That doesn't look good," Curtis deadpanned.

"Not hardly," Sibyl said in a low voice, without any trace of humor.

Jun raised her own T-99 to her shoulder so get a better look through the rifle's scope, and in the midst of that dust cloud she could see figures moving, and here and there lights could be glimpsed through the gloom.

"They are closing on our position," Werner added, unnecessarily.

Not only did the dust cloud grow larger as it neared, but sounds from within became increasingly audible. Inhuman whispering in unintelligible tongues. Shrieks that sounded like the screams of a person dying in a raging fire. The clattering of bone on bone, and of rotten flesh slapping against the ground with every footstep. It was an unearthly symphony of decay and death on the move.

"Okay, people," the sergeant called out, "we need to get these refugees to safety at base camp quickly. We don't have the food, water, or supplies for a long slog, even if we *could* manage to get clear of that mess of the Dead without them closing in around our flanks. So the only clear path to base camp is straight through those bastards…"

"Not all that 'clear,' sarge," Curtis muttered.

"The only path that gets us there at all in short order, then, does that suit you better?" The sergeant glared in the young American's direction until Curtis broke eye contact and stared at the ground beneath his feet. "We've got to fight through their lines, keeping the refugees safe and in one piece, and *soon*, and if there are any of the Dead bastards still straggling along behind us when we get to base camp, the defensive emplacements there will keep them off our backs."

"Why not just draw the line here and put them all down before we continue?" Jun asked. She didn't much look forward to the notion of escorting a group of terrified refugees through the teaming ranks of a horde of the enemy Dead.

"Because of *them*," the sergeant said simply, and nodded back in the direction that they'd come.

Jun glanced back, and saw another dust cloud to the north.

"They've been slowly advancing on us for the last quarter hour," the sergeant said, his voice level and restrained, but with an iron resolve beneath his words. "Didn't see much point in drawing y'all's attention to the bastards when it looked like we'd be easily outpacing them, but with this other group of bastards now blocking our way in front…"

He trailed off, with a vague shrug. His point was clear enough. The longer that the squad delayed in dealing with the horde of the Dead who were blocking the road to the south, the closer the horde pursuing them from the north would get to their rear flank. And wait too long, and they would run the risk of being completely surrounded and cut off.

"Very well, Josiah," Sibyl said, nodding in the sergeant's direction. "How best do you think that we should proceed, then?"

The sergeant slung his shotgun over his shoulder so that his hands were free. Then he held his arms in front of him, with his fingertips steepled together and his elbow held wide, forming a wide inverted "V" shape.

"Vanguard formation," he explained, motioning upwards with a quick movement of his arms, his steepled fingers driving upwards like the tip of a spear. "We don't have time for subtlety and nuance, so we need to hit them hard and fast and push through before they've got time to react. I'll take point. Sibyl and Werner, you flank me on either side, and Curtis and Jun, you two bring up the rear to the left and right. The refugees will stay inside the vanguard, huddled as close together and moving as fast as possible. Shotguns and submachine guns are the order of the day; rifles while there's still daylight between us and them, then switch to close quarters when we engage, mow the Dead down, and keep on moving. It doesn't even matter so much if you put the bastards down for good, so long as you slow them down long enough for us to drive these refugees through their lines."

"Shouldn't we close up the rear in a diamond formation?" Jun said after raising her hand like she was still back in antinecro training at the Woolwich barracks. "To cover our retreat once we're through?"

The sergeant thought for a brief moment and then shook his head.

"I like the shape of your thinking, kid, but time and speed are of the essence. Once we're on the other side of their lines, keep an eye on our six just in case any of those fast-moving suicide Dead are tailing us, but otherwise we should be able to outrun any of the garden-variety shamblers or skeletons that come our way."

As if to emphasize the sergeant's point, a scream broke forth from the roiling dust cloud in front of them, and one of the Dead came into view. It had a grenade clutched against its chest in one bony hand, and was sprinting towards the squad as quickly as its rotting limbs would carry it.

"Watch out!" the sergeant shouted as he unslung his Springfield in one quick motion, raised the barrel, and fired from the hip without having a chance to draw a bead on the target.

Long years of experience and well-worn instincts clearly won out, as the shot from the sergeant's rifle drove straight through the charging zombie's head, stopping it in its tracks. It staggered back, bony arm dropping to its side, the grenade slipping from its undead grasp as it began to fall. The pin pulled lose, seconds ticked by, and...

The grenade exploded, sending shrapnel hurling in every direction.

Jun and the others recoiled instinctively, even though they were just outside the blast radius of the grenade, thanks to the sergeant's timely shot.

"Nice shooting, sarge," Curtis said, after a low whistle.

The charging "suicide" Dead always unsettled Jun. And it wasn't just the inhuman shrieking sound they made as they charged, or the threat of imminent explosions that inevitably followed within moments of one of them making their presence known. It was the fact that they moved so much more quickly than the "shamblers" which the squad more commonly encountered, which the suicide Dead otherwise closely resembled. Even the anti-necro specialists who had trained Jun at Woolwich hadn't been able to explain precisely why ever since the start of the outbreak the one variety of Dead was able to move so much more quickly than the other, despite the overall similarities that they shared. It had been speculated that there was somehow a finite amount of movement that a reanimated body was capable of performing, a limited amount of energy that it could expend, and that the relatively slow pace of the typical shambler was conceivably a means by which to extend their usefulness on the battlefield as long as possible. By contrast, the suicide Dead were capable of moving at much greater rates of speed in order to deliver blindingly fast and unexpected attacks, but at the expense of long term viability. There had even been some debate amongst the more scientifically minded of Jun's instructors about potential experiments that could be performed in the field, for instance removing a grenade unexploded from the grip of a suicide Dead before they'd had the chance to complete their attack, and then see how much longer the undead remained upright and mobile afterwards. At the time, Jun had agreed that it was an interesting thought experiment...

But once she had gone first gone out on patrol with the deadhunter squad, it was clear to her why none of that type of hypothesis had ever been tested in field conditions. The first time a suicide Dead had charged at her, she had been only too eager to see the damned thing explode from as far a distance as she could manage, if only to put an end to its unearthly shrieking. The notion of disarming the fiend and then performing experiments on its subsequent mobility was the farthest thing from her mind.

Like at the moment, for example. Her thoughts were occupied by relief that the sergeant's shot had taken out the grenade-wielding Dead before it had closed on their position, and wary vigilance as she kept careful watch on the roiling dust cloud to make sure that another suicide zombie did not come charging towards them.

"Form up," the sergeant said, after Werner had translated his instructions for the refugees, who now huddled together even more tightly-packed at the center of the roadway. "It's now or never."

Jun took up her position on the trailing right flank of the vanguard, a few paces behind and to the right of Werner, who himself was behind and a few paces to the right of the sergeant who was at the forwardmost point of the arrow-head-shaped formation.

She glanced past the backs of the refugees in the rear of the pack, at Curtis who was in the mirror of her position on the trailing left flank of the formation.

"Somehow, I'm convinced this is still all your fault," Jun called out to him. "You were the one who said that we'd seen the last of the Dead on this mission, after all."

Curtis sighed wearily as he checked the magazine of his submachine gun and then raised its stock to his shoulder.

"You're probably right," he answered with a slight smile. "I should have known to keep my damn fool mouth shut, for once."

"Move out," the sergeant called from the head of the formation, driving towards the horde to their south.

"Cheer up, Jun," Curtis called back to her as they began to jog forward, keeping pace with the huddle of refugees. "I'm sure this'll be a piece of cake!"

Jun swore in Mandarin beneath her breath, hoping that Curtis hadn't tempted fate yet again...

CHAPTER 8

JUN KNEW A little bit about fighting battles against conventional forces. She grew up hearing stories about the massive battle for the provincial capital of Taiyuan, that put all of Shanxi province under Japanese occupation. She could remember the day that the Japanese forces first arrived to take control of her hometown of Datong, and the pitched battles that broke out as the Japanese fought to gain control of the few neighborhoods of holdouts that resisted their authority. She'd heard the old men quoting passages from Sun Tzu in intense conversations late at night in clandestine meetings in her parents' home, strategizing how they might regain control of their homes from the foreign invaders, as if reading a book could prepare them for waging an actual war.

But everything she knew about fighting against the living could be summed up in just a few key points, the most important of which was the principle of self-preservation. That is, that any enemy, no matter how devoted they might be to their cause, no matter how willing to put their own lives at risk, is still driven to one degree or another by the desire to survive the battle. Fighters who were so selfless as to throw themselves into combat without the slightest concern for their own well-being were so rare that they might as well be a dragon or phoenix or some other kind of mythological being, as the chances of encountering such a fighter in the world were just as likely as coming across a talking fish or a giant in your daily travels. The Japanese had trained fanatical pilots willing to crash their own planes into the sides of ships in order to sink enemy vessels, but that kind of devotion was carefully engrained, and the typical foot soldier in the Japanese army that Jun had observed growing up had not exhibited anything like that degree of zealousness. The Japanese forces who occupied Datong had all been clearly eager to return to their homes and families back in Japan when all was said and done. Sacrificing their lives needlessly in order to extend the occupation of an enemy territory for a day longer than was feasible was not high on the list of anyone's priorities.

That was the principal difference between fighting the living and fighting the Dead. The living fought to win, but also to survive. The Dead fought simply to destroy and to consume, whichever came first, and if the attempt came at the cost of their own destruction, then so be it. The Dead could not be intimidated by an overwhelming enemy force; they would continue to lurch and shriek towards the enemy so long as the ability to move forward remained in their rotting forms. No matter the odds in their favor the Dead would continue to follow their insatiable drives, come what may.

So if a horde of the Dead would not be deterred if facing an enemy force that outnumbered them by orders of magnitude, how much less concerned would they be by a squad of five deadhunters defending a dozen-and-a-half tired and terrified civilians?

The sergeant set the pace as the squad advanced. Quick, but not a sprint. Fast, but still slow to give the squad time to sight on individual targets as they advanced, as opposed to firing blindly into the mass before them. But most importantly, steady and relentless; they would not be giving up any ground, and every foot that they gained fighting forward, every inch of terrain that they covered, the squad would put behind them and continue onwards. There would be no retreat, not with a second horde of the Dead advancing on them from the north and getting closer by the moment.

From her position on the trailing right flank, Jun sighted through the telescopic scope of her T-99, picked out the glowing heart of another animated skeleton like the one who had attacked Curtis only a matter of moments before, and squeezed off a round. Her shot hit true, as evidenced by the muffled thump of an explosion followed by an expanding cloud of bone splinters, shredded cartilage, and desiccated viscera.

Jun could hear the voices of the refugees shuffling forward in the midst of the vanguard, muttering prayers in a babble of voices, calling on whatever divine forces might still be receptive to the pleas of the living to provide assistance.

Moving steadily forward, Jun swung the barrel of her rifle around, searching out another target. She didn't have to search for long. There was one of the Dead already emerging from the dissipating cloud of bone her last shot had produced, shambling forward through the remains of its undead brethren without any sign of recognition or acknowledgement. That was something else that separated the living from the Dead. The undead forces of the enemy would never pause to mourn a fallen comrade, never be spurred to rash action by the fall of another that they held dear. It was unknown whether the Dead held anything dear, for that matter, but that was more a philosophical point than a tactical one. Where a living opponent might be driven to act contrary to their own strategic advantage through grief or anger or the desire for vengeance, the Dead scarcely seemed to take any notice of losses on their side at all. Each of the Dead might just as well be an army of one advancing on a shared enemy, rather than a member of a larger force acting in unison.

But this, in its own way, was often an advantage for the living. A group of enemies composed of living, breathing, thinking soldiers could coordinate their efforts, opting to have one member of the team take point and others to defend the rear, just as Jun and the rest of the squad were doing now. But a group of the Dead were all driven by the same naked appetites and instincts, each of them individually propelled forward by the desire to satiate their insatiable hungers. There had been times when fighting the Dead on the Eastern Front that this bit of wisdom had come in handy for Jun, as she had positioned herself at the mouth of a chokepoint through which only one body could pass at a time. The enemy Dead would crowd the other side, pushing against one another ceaselessly in their attempt to break through to the other side where light and life beaconed to them, leaving Jun free to fire on them one-by-one as they tried to squeeze through the narrow opening. There were times when she had managed to plug a breech in the wall with the bodies of the fallen enemy themselves, at least until the fallen Dead began to quickly decay.

To her left and a few paces ahead, Jun could hear Werner's MP40 barking in his hands, firing round after round into the horde advancing towards them. In battle, any indecision or awkwardness that might occasionally be glimpsed in the German's manner in peaceful moments was long forgotten: he executed each maneuver flawlessly, placing every shot where it would do the most strategic damage, selecting his targets with expert care and precision.

Jun squeezed the trigger of her T-99, taking a moment's grim satisfaction in seeing the head of one of the shambling Dead exploding into mist, then working the bolt of the rifle to chamber another round and selecting her next target.

Lights burned deep within the cloud of dust, and before Jun could fire another round a burning figure burst forward into clear view, limbs flailing as it shrieked a horrifying scream and came charging towards the vanguard.

Jun was flustered, having had close calls with the fire zombies on several occasions. She swung around her rifle's barrel, her heart in her throat, and fired off a round...

The round went wide, missing the head of the burning figure by several inches. The burning figure raced forward, mouth open wide in an inhuman howl.

Hands trembling, Jun struggled to work the action of her rifle's bolt again, but her fingers slipped and her palm jammed down hard against the rounded end of the bolt. Cursing in Mandarin, she shook her hand, and tried again to take hold of the bolt. Only seconds remained until...

From her left came the sudden bark of Werner's MP40 and the burning zombie's head exploded just instants before its entire body collapsed into a pile of ash on the ground.

Jun chanced a quick glance in Werner's direction, and the German soldier gave her an abbreviated nod before turning his attention back to the horde of Dead charging towards them.

Swallowing hard and collecting her wits, Jun worked the bolt to chamber another round in her rifle, took a deep breath, and then sighted her next target.

She only got off a single round more with her rifle before she heard the sergeant shouting from the head of the vanguard.

"Close quarters!" the sergeant called out. "Mow the bastards down!"

Jun's gaze darted in his direction, and she could see that the leading point of the vanguard was now almost within arm's reach of the forward-most of the horde. She slung the T-99 over her shoulder and limbered up her Thompson submachine gun.

Jun fired a burst of submachine gun fire at a shambling Dead who threaten to drive through the narrow gap between herself and Werner, and then took a step over its headless and already rotting corpse without missing a beat. As she did so, the Dead who had been following in the shambler's wake were still shambling towards the spot that she'd just vacated, and were now having to turn their lumbering attentions towards the spot that she had advanced into.

This was another of the instances in which the enemy Dead's mindless drives could be used to the advantage of the living. The Dead were forever driven to shamble or shriek or hurtle towards the place where their living prey was in that precise moment. They could not strategize or plan ahead, moving instead to intercept their prey where it would shortly be, instead. So that even in the midst of a large number of enemy Dead, the living could still work this to their advantage if they simply kept moving. Aim for the head or the heart, scan for incoming, and keep moving.

In a scrum such as this, of course, there were the grasping hands to contend with, to say nothing of the deafening shrieks and the noxious scent of rotting flesh. But the basic principle remained the same.

Jun was directing a spray of fire across a wide arc before her when one of the shamblers, stumbling forward on two stumps of legs that each ended at the knee, managed to grab hold of her right arm. The Dead managed to yank her right hand away from the trigger of her Thompson M1A1, and was dragging the arm towards its own yawning maw, teeth gnashing as its rotting jaw worked furiously in its ruined mouth.

For the briefest of instants, barely the duration of a heartbeat, Jun felt a momentary panic. This was familiar, too, in a far less pleasant way. She remembered the sounds of her friends and colleagues in Moscow screaming as the rising tide of the Dead had dragged them under, and the feeling of helplessness that had overwhelmed her as she watched them go, unable to save them. For that brief heartbeat, she could feel that same sense of helplessness threatening to rise up and overtake her, as she struggled fruitlessly to drag her arm from the shambler's vicelike grip.

Then that helpless feeling was squashed down as an iron resolve settled over her like a suit of armor, and she gritted her teeth in barely control fury.

"Let *go!*" she shouted as she swung around the stock of the Thompson in her left hand and bashed it into the side of the shambler's skull. The submachine gun's stock slammed into the Dead's head with a sickening thud and a crack, but still the Dead maintained its grip on her arm.

The vanguard was advancing. Jun could see the rearmost of the refugees from the corner of her eye, their backs to her as they huddled together and shuffled forward in the sergeant's wake. If Jun was not able to keep pace with them and defend the vanguard's right flank, then the Dead would be free to approach and attack from the rear.

Jun referred to the shambler grappling her with a Mandarin obscenity that would have shocked her mother to hear, and then brought the stock of the Thompson crashing down onto the skull of the Dead, and again, and again. A deep rage had risen up from deep within Jun, and her vision went red as she continued to bash in the shambler's skull again and again and again, and still its desiccated claw of a hand continued to grip her arm.

"Jun!" the voice of Werner broke through the red haze, shaking her out of her violent reverie. "On your right!"

She looked down and realized that the hand which gripped her right arm was no longer attached to a body, as the Dead who had grappled her had collapsed in a heap on the ground, its forearm snapping off in the process. She shook the severed limb off her just in time to swing her submachine gun back in line and fire at the next undead shambler who was approaching from her right.

As the next Dead fell in a heap Jun moved quickly it until she regained her position at the trailing edge of the vanguard. She didn't know if the refugees had noticed her absence behind them or not.

The zombies who had been shambling towards her previous position were in the process of changing course and heading towards the ground that Jun now occupied, but she didn't intend to stick around long enough for any of them to catch up. A few carefully placed bursts from her Thompson cleared a path ahead and to the right of her current position as the vanguard climbed over the bodies that had fallen before them, already rotting to putrescence beneath their feet, the smell of foul decay thick in the air. The echoes of gun fire and shotgun blasts echoed all around them, as the members of the deadhunter squad carried out their grim mission without hesitation.

Jun was in the process of swapping out the now-empty drum magazine for her submachine gun with a full one, hurrying lest one of the faster moving zombies managed to close the distance to her before she was through, and then swung the barrel up and sighted for her next target. It was only then that she realized that there were no more of the Dead remaining in front of the vanguard, only behind them. They had broken through the line of the undead horde and were now completely on the other side.

"Double time!" shouted Sergeant Josiah from the lead of the vanguard. "Flat out until we make base camp!"

The vanguard took off in a sprint down the road, with Jun and Curtis in the rear drifting closer together, closing in behind the rear of the refugees, covering them from any attack from behind.

"See? What'd I tell 'ya?" Curtis said, slowing down for a brief moment to fire a round from his M1 Carbine at one of the glowing heart of a skeleton who was racing towards them from behind, bony limbs flailing. His shot hit its mark, and the skeleton erupted into a bloom of splintered bone. It was as if he was trying to wash away any memory of the way that the skeleton that had burst from the ground only a short while before had made him a frantic mess for a short while. "A piece of cake."

From the far corner of the horde one of the suicide zombies came charging towards them, grenade clasped to its hollow chest, a horrible shriek issuing from its wide-open maw. Curtis recoiled in panic, fumbling with his M1, almost dropping it in the process.

With cool precision, Jun drew her Webley from its holster, sighted along its barrel, and planted a round dead square in the suicide zombie's forehead. It toppled, arms falling to its side and its grip on the grenade loosening.

"Right," Jun said with a sidelong glance in Curtis's direction as he watched wide-eyed as the grenade exploded, sending bits of rotten flesh and bone fragments flying in all directions. Curtis had developed a kind of phobia of the suicide zombies ever since one of them nearly detonated right in his face a couple of months earlier, and now he seemed to lose all composure if suddenly presented with one without warning. "Now come on, you heard the sergeant, let's get moving!"

CHAPTER 9

THE SUN WAS just beginning to set behind the western horizon. The undead horde that the sergeant had driven the vanguard through still trailed them, followed not far behind by the second horde that had been following some distance to the north, and if Jun and the others were to stop advancing them the Dead who remained up and ambulatory would be on them with grasping hands and biting jaws in a matter of moments. So it was a considerable sense of relief when they caught sight of the stockade fence around their base camp, rising to the south, with electrical spotlights shining brightly from poles high atop the corners of the fence, and a second wire fence encircling the whole camp at a distance of a dozen paces or so.

Jun was eager to get behind the safety of those walls. They had been travelling since sunup with only the one brief rest in the afternoon, and had been moving as fast as their legs would carry them since breaking through the horde of the undead the better part of an hour before. And none too soon, as the refugees that they were escorting seemed barely able to stay upright. Not that Jun wasn't in sore need of a rest herself. The idea of setting down her weapons and her pack, or sitting herself down somewhere… She paused, sighing deeply at the thought of unlacing her boots and stretching out her bare feet for a while. It feel like ages since she had last had a chance to wash up and properly relax for a moment.

But so long as they remained exposed and out in the open, she couldn't drop her guard even for an instant. All it would take was a single undead menace bursting from the ground beneath her after she'd put down her weapons and put up her feet, and her long battle against the forces of the Dead would finally be at an end, and not in a good way.

"Anybody home?" the sergeant called up to the watch tower that rose above the stockade fence. They were only a short distance from the gate, and by now they should have been issued a challenge by the guards on watch. But while a spotlight shone from its swivel mount atop the watch tower, its beam was not pointed at the approaching vanguard on the road, but was instead directed aimlessly off into the night sky. So unless the guards were watchful of airborne zombies winging their way towards the camp, then it seemed that the approaches were not being covered.

Jun found herself wondering about the possibilities of there actually being airborne Dead, and already beginning to formulate possible strategic defenses against them when a voice called down from the watchtower above.

"Who's that, then?" It sounded like whoever was up in the tower had just been rousted from a deep sleep.

Jun was still thinking about how best to defend oneself against an undead menace attacking from the air. It was an unconscious habit she had of dealing with nervous energy, or of staving off fatigue; come up with a hypothetical, and then perseverate on possible solutions until some other productive task presented itself to her. Her eyes and ears remained open to her surroundings, wary of any encroaching threat, but her conscious thoughts busied themselves with trivial speculations.

The sergeant was identifying himself and the rest of the squad.

"And we've got a group of refugees down off the mountains, civilians in need of medical attention and secure lodgings."

There was a hushed exchange that took place atop the tower for several moments, a back and forth that registered as nothing more than a susurration by the time it reached Jun's ears, and then she could hear the reinforced gate in the stockade fence beginning to be cranked open.

"Okay, you're clear to enter," the voice called down from the watchtower. "But be quick about it, looks like you've got Dead on your tail."

"We know *that*, jackass," Curtis snarled in the direction of the tower as they ushered the refugees in through the gate and into the security of the base camp. "Who the heck do you think we've been saving these poor bastards from this whole time?"

The refugees all seemed shell-shocked after the events of the day, and their reprieve time and again from the nameless undead who seemed to hound their heels. They scarcely even spoke now, seemed hardly to react to their surroundings, but simply moved in the direction that the sergeant told them to, stopped when he said to stop, spoke only when he fired questions directly at them.

Once the last of the refugees was safely inside and Curtis and Jun had made it through the gate, the sergeant signaled up to the watchtower for the gate to be closed again. As the gate began to creak shut, Jun saw one of the tower guards descending a ladder that was attached to the side of the tower facing the interior of the camp, a rifle slung across his back and binoculars hanging from his neck.

He wore the uniform of a major in the British infantry, with a battered beret atop his head and the yellow armband of the original Survivors Brigade wound around his upper arm. It signified that he was one of the combatants who had been in the battlefield fighting the last war when the Dead had first climbed from their graves and the surviving members of all of the living armies on both sides of the old conflict had been forced to set aside their differences and fight together for the living.

Most of the Resistance fighters who Jun had served with since transferring from Woolwich to Reclamation Zone Italia had been newcomers like herself, who had only recently joined the effort long after the Dead War had already begun; or else they were soldiers like Werner and Curtis who had served out the last days of the previous war in some form of ignominy, prisoners of war or members of penal battalions; or they were volunteer like Sergeant Josiah and Sibyl, who had been civilian adventurers of one form or another before the outbreak of the Dead War, but who now served within a paramilitary chain of command. It was rare to encounter someone who wore the sign of the original Survivors Brigade so prominently, in large part because the death toll in those early days of the Dead War had been so high, and there were precious few of those initial resistance fighters still among the living.

But the British major who was now striding from the base of the watchtower towards them was clearly on this side of the grave, hale and hearty, with a thick bushy mustache, full cheeks, and a bright, lively, sky-blue eyes. He looked as though he'd just woken up from a long nap, which to every indication was precisely what had happened.

"Good to see you, old boy," the major said, shaking hands with Josiah. "We expected you back day before last, and when you didn't turn up we'd begun to expect the worst."

"Good to be back, sir," the sergeant replied, wearing a weary smile. "It's been awhile."

Major Wilkins had been the ranking officer at the base camp when Jun's squad had first been posted here, overseeing a busting crew of subordinates who provided rear echelon support for squads of deadhunters clearing out this whole region of Northern Italy. But aside from the pair of subalterns who were wearily cranking the reinforced gate in the fence shut, and a lone medical officer who was heading out of the nearest of the Quonset huts with a first aid kit under his arm, walking briskly in the direction of the refugees, there didn't seem to be any other Resistance personnel in evidence in the camp. It was too early for everyone to be sleeping, with the sun still pinking the western sky. So where was everybody?

It had been some time since the squad had last been in the camp, after all. They'd been working their way through the countryside checking off reference numbers on that old survey map for the better part of a month. And they'd only been in the camp a day or two then, stopping in briefly to refuel and refresh for a short while after finishing their previous tour and the last set of coordinates that they'd been sent out to check and reference numbers to cross off of a list.

But in the just more than three weeks that the squad had been out in the field, the basecamp appeared to have been emptied out almost completely.

The sergeant was giving the major a more detailed summary of how the squad had encountered the group of refugees fleeing down out of the southern foothills of the Alps almost two days before, and had just reached the point in the account where he was about to relate what the refugees had told them about the Nazis' Alpine Fortress when the Major held up his hand and signaled for silence.

"You are due for a proper debriefing and I am overdue for my evening meal," the major said, a smile tugging up the corners of his mouth and with a twinkle in his eye. "Let's kill two birds with one stone, shall we?"

He gestured towards a large canvas tent that was used as the camp's mess.

"Join me for dinner, will you? We're a bit short staffed at the canteen, but I'm sure we can find something that will suit our needs."

The sergeant glanced around at Jun and the others, none of whom could muster the energy to do much more than nod.

"After you, sir," the sergeant replied. "But if you don't mind me asking, where the heck *is* everybody?"

The major was already leading the way to the mess tent, and when he glanced over his shoulder to look in the squad's direction Jun could see the good humor leeching from his face.

"Thereby hangs a tale, son," he said.

From the other side of the stockade fence could be heard the sound of the Dead horde approaching, finally catching up with the squad after pursuing them more than an hour.

"Man the tower," the major called over to the subalterns who had just finished securing the gate. "Electrify the defensive perimeter, and take out any of the blighters who make it through to the inner fence." He paused, and then added with emphasis, "But don't waste any shots, you hear me? Ammunition is running low enough as it is."

A switch was thrown, and with a crackle and pop the outer wire fence that encircled the camp was suddenly humming with a high voltage electrical charge. It would be enough to deter any of the Dead who ventured too close, or so Jun hoped. Because if the Resistance was worrying about running low on ammunition to the extent that they were picking and choosing which of the encroaching zombies to shoot? Then things might have gotten more dire than she had realized.

A second medical officer had come out of the Quonset hut that served as the camp's makeshift hospital, and together with the one who had carried out the first aid kit was in the process of escorting the refugees inside to be examined, cleaned up as well as practicable, and then presumably someone would find temporary accommodations for them.

The major had reached the entrance to the mess tent, and was holding the flap open for Josiah and the rest of the squad to enter, like a maître d' at a posh restaurant showing a party of diners to their table.

From the other side of the stockade fence Jun could hear a sudden peal of inhuman screeching, like the howling shrieks of the damned and tormented, accompanied by a crackling sizzle as the first of the pursuing shamblers in the horde of Dead reached the electrified fence.

"Come along now," the major urged, gesturing to the tent's entrance with his free hand, the other still holding the flap open. "Soup's on."

The smell of burning hair and scorched meat reached Jun's nostrils, with undertones of putrefaction and decay, and the agonized howls from beyond the stockade still echoed through the twilight as she stepped past the major and into the tent. And as soon as she stepped inside, she caught the scent of the hearty stew that she had last enjoyed when they had billeted in the base camp before going out on their most recent deployment, and Jun's mouth watered as her stomach growled in response. That the scent of the electrified Dead still lingering in her nostrils did nothing to hinder her appetites suggested things about the ways in which her experiences were affecting her that Jun was not interested in dwelling on for the time being. She was hungrier than she had realized, and whether

she satiated that hunger or not had no bearing on
the undead beyond the walls of the camp...

CHAPTER 10

As UNUSUAL AS it had been to see Major Wilkins acting like a maître d' at a restaurant as he ushered the squad into the mess tent, it was even stranger to see him acting as a server as he helped the camp cook ladle portions of the stew out into metal bowls for Jun and the rest of the squad, before serving himself and then joining them at the table. At least the major opted to sit at the head of the table, so some degree of hierarchy and decorum was preserved.

Jun wasn't the only one taken aback by the major's willingness to pitch in and assist with tasks that might otherwise be considered to be beneath his station. Both Werner and Josiah's faces registered surprise, and even Curtis, who was normally the last to stand on ceremony and who had very little time for custom and hierarchies in general, seemed a little flustered as he accepted the bowl of stew ladled out for him by the ranking officer. Of all of the squad only Sibyl seemed to take the major's participation in menial labor in her stride without any outward sign of surprise or confusion.

Sibyl apparently did take note of the surprise evident in Jun's own expression, however. As Jun sat with a metal spoon full of stew held halfway to her mouth, her gaze fixed on the major seated at the far end of the table, the Englishwoman leaned in close to her and spoke in a low voice.

"Eat up, dear," Sibyl said with a sly smile, and then glanced around at their squad mates who were eagerly tucking into their own bowls. "Wait too much longer and one of these big strapping men is likely to eat the bowl for you."

Sheepishly, Jun took the bite, chewing on a gristly bit for a moment, averting her eyes and staring down as she idly stirred her bowl of stew with the spoon.

"It's like my Chester always used to say, dear," Sibyl added quietly in a conspiratorial tone. "The true mark of a leader is the willingness to muck in and do whatever job needs doing, rather than lording over things from on high and afraid to get one's hands dirty."

As if in response, the major cleared his throat, and dabbed at the corners of his mouth with a handkerchief before addressing the squad in general, and Sergeant Josiah in particular.

"Now, as I said, I'm very pleased to have you lot back in the fold, dear boy," he began, stroking his bushy mustache. "There have been significant developments since your squad was sent out into the field last month, and the landscape is moving beneath our feet, as it were. And I'm sorry to say that it means that your squad will be back out in the field sooner rather than later." He paused, meaningfully, and added, "*Much* sooner."

Sergeant Josiah glanced around the table at Jun and the others, gauging their reactions. Curtis was rolling his eyes while Sibyl sighed dramatically, while Werner carried on eating his stew with a studied lack of interest in anything other than his evening meal. Jun just hoped that they'd get a chance to catch a full night's rest before going back out on patrol, and only her ingrained need to follow the chain of command restrained her from saying as much out loud.

"Sir, you don't mind me asking...?" the sergeant began, and gestured back towards the tent's entrance, indicating the rest of the base camp beyond. "This place is damn near empty. There's usually at least a couple of deadhunter squads taking a little downtime between operations, support staff, you name it. Where the heck did everybody go?"

The major nodded slowly as he sighed heavily.

"As I say, the landscape has shifted, and we are shifted along with it," Major Wilkins replied, wearily. "We thought that we were in the final stages of reclaiming this portion of the continent, with only a cleanup effort remaining, such as the operation you lot have been on these past weeks. But then we began to see a sudden sharp increase in the pace of Dead sightings, starting in the northeast corner of our zone and continuing south and west as the days progressed. Isolated cases at first—lone roamers and small packs of shamblers, mostly—but increasingly squads were returning with reports of encountering full hordes of the wretched things."

"We run across three different groupings of the bastards in as many days." Josiah's tone was flat and controlled, but Jun could hear the simmering anger beneath his words. For all of his easygoing good humor, she knew that the sergeant harbored a deep animosity against the Dead that went far beyond the demands of his present duties. "Put down as many of them as we could, but there's more of 'em still wandering around out there."

"My point exactly, old boy," the major answered,

like a teacher pleased that one of his students had given the correct response to a difficult question. "And we have received an ever growing number of requests for urgent aid from the few remaining inhabited settlements in the region—most of the residents of the towns and villages in the surrounding countryside fled south at the outbreak of the Dead War and are still sheltering across the water in Sicily, but those stubborn holdouts who remained look to us to protect them against the onslaught of the Dead menace. And so any deadhunter squads on hand were dispatched without delay, and any of the squads who returned from cleanup missions have been sent right back out into the field as quickly as possible. Then there came that unpleasant business last week…"

The major trailed off into silence for a moment, a pained expression flashing across his face as he turned and stared off into the middle distance. Then he seemed to regain his composure by sheer force of will, bit by bit, finally turning his attention back to the squad before him.

"The generator conked out and a whole horde of the Dead made it to the fence while the electrical defenses were down," he said matter-of-factly, as though he were discussing the weather and describing a time that it had rained particularly hard. "We managed to pick off most of them from the watch towers, but a few of them made it over the wall and…"

The major's voice choked in his throat for a moment, his jaw tightening and his eyes narrowed into slits.

"Casualties were kept to a minimum, but even so…" He paused, taking a deep breath in through his nostrils, and then holding it for a long moment before exhaling slowly. "In any event, the threat was neutralized and the camp's defenses were strengthened in response, but as a result we are considerably short-handed. As you can clearly see, eh?"

Jun glanced around the table, and saw that like her, the others were clearly unsure how to respond, or if in fact they should.

After a brief awkward silence in which it was unclear whether the major was waiting for some sort of response from the squad in general or the sergeant in particular, or was instead simply collecting his thoughts before continuing, he suddenly cleared his throat loudly, sat up straighter, and slammed a fist on the surface of the table.

"The level of incursion that we are experiencing is the highest it has been in the region at any point since the beginning of the Dead War," the major said, his voice raised, his manner urgent. "And at a point where we had allowed ourselves to believe that we were beginning to beat back the undead menace in this region. So the question that lies before us is, What can possibly explain this sudden surge in enemy activity? Is there some new source of Dead troops about which we are as yet unaware? We should be approaching the point of absolute victory in the region and yet instead we find ourselves fighting a holding action, and running the risk of losing ground in the process."

Major Wilkins slammed his fist down onto the table again, even harder this time, and the metal bowl in front of Jun rocked and wobbled in response, sending stew flying out onto the table's surface.

"If we only knew where the blighters were coming from!" the major shouted, spittle flying from his mouth, catching in the corners of his mustache.

Sergeant Josiah glanced over at Jun and the others, and she could see that he was thinking the same thing that she and no doubt the rest of their squad mates was thinking at that exact moment.

"Sir," the sergeant began gingerly, as if dealing with unexploded ordnance and worried that it might go off in his face, "like I was saying, about the refugees come down out of the mountains?"

The major turned and gave Josiah a hard stare.

"Poor devils," the major finally replied. "Seemed scared half out of their wits. It was a lucky thing, them running into you lot like they did. And you say they had fled from somewhere up in the Alps?"

"From all over the place, actually, but it was a party of them from one village in particular that... Well, Mr. Sauer here was the one who was the one who was able to talk with all of 'em," he turned and gestured in Werner's direction, "so maybe he could do a better job of telling you just what it was they'd said."

The major turned his attention in Werner's direction. The German soldier was in the process of polishing off his bowl of stew, carefully scrapping his spoon around the inner curve of the bowl to get every last bit of sustenance out that he could manage.

"Well?" the major said, beginning to sound a little impatient.

Werner glanced up from his now empty bowl, cocking one eyebrow in a quizzical expression. Jun noted that the sergeant hadn't actually directly ordered Werner to give the major his account yet, and couldn't help wondering whether he wasn't simply being a stickler for rules. Werner was a loyal soldier, and would speak if ordered to, but as Josiah had framed his statement more along the lines of a hypothetical, Werner was not disobeying orders to concentrate on finishing his dinner first.

"Tell the man what you told us already, Werner," the sergeant finally clarified, more than a touch exasperated.

Werner carefully set his spoon down beside his bowl, then pushed his chair back from the table and climbed to his feet. Standing at attention, with his gaze directed somewhere just above the top of the major's beret, he began to recount what the fleeing villagers had told him.

As Werner talked about the Nazis moving men and materials through the mountains that last winter of the war, Jun glanced around the mess tent. In the time that she and her squad had been sitting there and eating, a handful of other residents of the camp had drifted in and taken up positions at other tables scattered around the interior of the tent. Jun recognized one of the medical officers who had escorted the refugees away, and who was now sitting with a beleaguered expression on her face and shoulders slumped as she stared into a steaming hot cup of tea with a faraway look in her eye. At the next table over was a man with a neatly-trimmed mustache wearing a flight suit, chuckling to himself as he read a sheaf of typewritten letters and made his leisurely way through a bowl of stew. Finally, at a table on the far side of the tent sat a pair of workers in coveralls, a man and a woman, who from the amount of dirt on their clothing and in their hair had spent the day digging a hole, filling a hole in, or both.

None of the newcomers had paid much mind to Jun and the rest of the squad as they entered the mess tent, and for a time each of them had seemed content to eat their evening meals in peace without taking any particular notice of what was being said at the central table with Jun's squad and the major. But as Werner continued his account of the reports of the Alpine Fortress, and the villagers' fears about an army of the Dead under the direct command of the SS officer Standartenführer Ziegler, he gradually captured the attention of the other diners in the tent. The medical officer was the first to be obviously engaged in what the German soldier was relating, quickly giving him her full and undivided attention, and Jun couldn't help wondering whether the medical officer had heard fragments of those same accounts from the refugees that she had seen to a short time before in the medical Quonset hut. Then the two ditch diggers gradually stopped exchanging verbal jabs and fell silent as they listened to what Werner was saying. The man with the well-trimmed mustache and the flight suit was the last to resist the lure of Werner's description of a secret Nazi fortress high in the mountains and the army of the Dead supposedly controlled from there, but even the pilot eventually turned his attention away from the letters he had been reading and sat in attentive silence as he eavesdropped on Werner's report.

For his part, Major Wilkins had been listening to Werner relate the stories he'd gathered from the refugees in relative silence, only once or twice asking a brief question or requesting a slight bit of clarification. Jun wondered whether it was simply a question of Werner giving a fairly exhaustive and detailed account to begin with—and she had to admit that he had gone into considerable detail—or whether the major was withholding any kind of judgement or assessment on his part until after he'd heard the German soldier's full account. She'd had only limited interactions with the major before, and almost always in situations where the camp's ranking officer had dealt with one of Jun's superior officers in her presence or address her simply as part of a larger group. She didn't have a strong sense of him as an individual, nor did she know him well enough to make any judgements or assumptions about his abilities and aptitudes as a leader. Earlier in their conversation he had seemed more weary than anything, seeming to still be mourning the loss of the personnel who had died in the course of the recent incursion of the Dead, or else struggling with feelings of guilt and remorse that the incursion had happened on his watch— or possibly both. But then Werner concluded his report on the rumored Alpine Fortress and, after clicking his heels together and bobbing his upper body forward in a brief motion in a kind of abbreviated bow, returned to his seat, and Jun and the others sat quietly watching the major sitting in silence at the far end of the table, his expression unreadable.

The entire mess tent seemed to sit blanketed under a pall of silence, all eyes on the major. Jun wondered whether the permanent residents of the camp knew something about the ranking officer that she didn't. Was he the type of leader given to even more violent outbursts than occasionally slamming his fist onto tables, despite an otherwise placid exterior? Back home in Datong there had been a block captain who often behaved in just that sort of fashion, seeming the picture of decorum and propriety in most situations but then flying into a spittle-flicking rage when things didn't unfold exactly as he had foreseen. After the Japanese withdrawal from the city he had been almost entirely unbearable, insisting that his neighbors follow his every suggestion and direction as the city began slowly to work out some semblance of self-governance after years of occupation. But he had been struck down by a heart attack soon after, and thankfully those who succeeded him in leadership positions in the neighborhood tended to be a little more adaptable and flexible in their outlooks than he had.

Because, even more than in any conventional conflict, the war between the living and the Dead required flexibility and the ability to adapt to changing circumstances quickly. When the enemy could burst forth from the ground beneath your feet without warning, or burst into flames as they rushed your position, or continue advancing despite a hail of bullets tearing the very flesh from their bones, a leader who was not prone to rigid ways of thinking and hidebound adherence to traditional ways of waging war was almost always preferable.

For a passing instant Jun feared the worst, and braced herself for some sort of outburst. But when the major finally spoke he put her fears to rest.

"Sergeant, I want you and your squad to get a

good night's rest," he began, calm and collected, pushing his chair back from the table and climbing to his feet. "You should find ample room to billet in the barracks. Then you are all to report to me for a briefing at oh eight hundred hours, after which you'll be resupplied by the quartermaster before heading out on your next mission."

"Sir?" Josiah said, a little perplexed. "What mission would that be, now?"

The major nodded in Werner's direction.

"If this supposed Alpine Redoubt *does* exist and the bloody-handed bastard running the show there has somehow managed to figure out how to command the movements of the Dead, then that just might be the answer that we've been looking for. Both to the question of where all of these ruddy Dead blighters are coming from, and what we can do to put a stop to it."

The major took in the blank stares from the sergeant and the rest of the others, then rolled his eyes towards the ceiling before continuing.

"If that blasted mountain fortress is there, then I need someone to find the bloody place and deal with it, once and for all. But as I said, we're short-handed, and all of the other deadhunters squads are already out in the field," he said like they were some sort of simpletons and he was explaining a blindingly obvious point, then gestured to the whole squad with a broad sweep of his hands. "So *you* lot are going to have to take care of it, obviously. So sleep well, and show up bright and early, ready to steal a march on the Dead!"

After the major had turned on his heel and marked out of the mess tent, Josiah glanced over at Jun and the rest of the squad, one eyebrow raised, gauging their reactions.

"Could be worse," Jun said, shrugging, "at least we're getting a good night's rest out of the deal."

CHAPTER 11

THE SQUAD ALL slept in the same barracks that night, with no divisions observed amongst them with regards to sex or rank. Each member of the squad got their own bunk in the barracks—and Jun tried not to think too long or too hard about whether the previous occupants of those bunks were simply out on patrol, or buried in a communal grave at the rear of the camp, or worse—which was the height of luxury compared to their typical accommodations while on maneuvers. Curtis snored, Sibyl talked in her sleep, and Josiah tossed and turned all night in the throes of some long-running nightmare, but Jun managed to tune all of them out in short order and fell into a deep, blissfully dreamless sleep.

She woke in the still dark hours of the morning to the sound of a low thrumming coming from somewhere outside the barracks, like the ceaseless growl of some enormous beast, or the buzz of an impossibly large swarm of bees. Jun went from drowsy bemusement to being alert and alarmed as she sat bolt upright on the bunk, trying to identify the sound she was hearing. Were they under attack?

Then she heard the thrumming sound change in pitch, rising first up sharply and then dropping steadily down in an increasingly low register. And it was then that she realized what she was hearing, and breathed a sigh of relief as she scolded herself for failing to recognize it sooner.

"Goddamn annoying planes," Curtis muttered from the bunk beside her without sitting up or even opening his eyes.

There was a small airfield attached to the basecamp, used primarily for small craft ferrying supplies and personnel from the larger installations in the southern reaches of the country to these outposts dotted across the north. But it was also home to a small fleet of planes used to survey the countryside from the air on a routine basis, as well as a staging ground for bombing fleets such as the one which had decimated the nameless village in the shadows of the Alps where the squad had first encountered the band of refugees. The sound that had awoken Jun was the noise of the planes' engines as the dawn patrol took off for their morning scouting run.

"Come on, y'all," the sergeant said, swinging his legs over the side of his bunk and reaching for his boots. "That's enough lollygagging, we've got work to do."

Werner was already on his feet, a washcloth draped over his left forearm and his shaving kit held in his right hand, heading towards the row of jury-rigged buckets that served as sinks that lined the rear of the Quonset hut. Curtis was still lying flat with one arm draped over his eyes, moaning slightly. Sibyl was still in her bunk as well, but had pushed herself up onto one elbow, gazing around the largely empty room.

"I suppose that breakfast in bed is out of the question," the Englishwoman said with a lopsided smile. "Room service in these places is just dreadful, isn't it?"

"I am just glad not to be sleeping on the ground for once," Jun said, as she reached under her bunch and pulled out the rucksack in which she kept her toiletry items. She stretched her shoulders, hands probing the small of her back, wincing slightly as she did. "I think I can still feel the rocks from that horrible little hillside we slept on last week?"

"You might just come to miss that hillside yet, kid," the sergeant called over, shaking his head.

"From the sound of it, the nights to come ain't going to be anywhere near as comfortable as those rocks were."

Curtis pushed himself up off his bunk with an overly dramatic groan, and rubbed the sleep from his eyes. "Any chance that major was joking last night, sarge? I mean, about sending us up the side of a damned mountain?"

"I didn't hear anyone laughing, Curtis," the sergeant said with a slight grin, "did you?"

"Nah," the young American groaned again, shaking his head, "but just 'cause it wasn't funny doesn't mean he was kidding us. I mean, as jokes go it's not really much of one, but that would make a whole hell of a lot more sense than him being serious about it."

"What's so hard to understand about it?" The sergeant sounded genuinely confused.

"Well, for one…" Curtis gestured broadly with both hands pointed towards the ceiling of the barracks. "Mountains?!"

The sergeant shrugged. "What of it?"

"He has a point, Josiah," Sibyl put in without looking up, crouched down by the side of her bunk and apparently in the midst of organizing the contents of her rucksack. Jun always marveled at the sheer volume of personal items that the

Englishwoman managed to fit into her backpack—keepsakes and mementos, cosmetics and sanitary materials, emergency rations and expensive candies—both in terms of her ability to cram so much into so small a space, and her capacity to carry it around all day without collapsing under the weight.

"How's that, now?" Sergeant Josiah arched an eyebrow, giving her a sidelong glance.

Sibyl put down a pocket knife, a wrist watch, and a tube of lipstick on the edge of her bunk before straightening up and turning to give the sergeant her undivided attention. "How many mountains have you climbed, hmm?"

"Well," the sergeant began, crossing his arms and sighing, "there was one time in Yokohama when the ship's quartermaster and I got mixed up with this pair of geishas on the run from a bunch of gangsters, and they chased us clear up the side of..."

Sibyl held up one hand to signal him to pause, a stern expression on her face like that of a teacher upon hearing an outlandish story about a student's homework being eaten by the family dog.

"Not one of your tall tales or fabulations, Josiah," she said, even tempered but with steel beneath her words. "Have you ever climbed a mountain?" She paused, and then added, "A *proper* mountain, not just a hill scarcely worthy of the name."

The sergeant scratched his chin

"I knew this Cajun fella back home who bet me that I couldn't…"

Sibyl sighed loudly, shaking her head.

"We are not spinning tales around the campfire," she said, exasperated. "A mountain does not care about your bluster or your bravado. The peaks of the world's tallest mountains are littered with the bodies of all those who attempted to scale the heights without the requisite skill, equipment, and blind luck to succeed in the attempt. So bearing in mind that what we are discussing, even in the hypothetical, would be a matter of life and death as grave as any of the undead menaces we face on a daily basis, I ask you one last time: have you ever climbed a mountain?"

Sergeant Josiah scowled for a moment, then shook his head. "No, I don't reckon that I have, ma'am."

"Well, I *have*," Sibyl shot back, eyes narrowed. "Several of them, as it happens, and on several continents at that. In fact, before the war Chester and I attempted to ascend to the top of Tirich Mir, the highest mountain in the Hindu Kush range of the Himalayas. Trained for weeks with our sherpa, a charming gentleman named Tenzing Norgay, and would likely have reached the summit if the weather had been in our favor. As it was we very nearly didn't make it back down in one piece, and if not for Mr. Norgay's expertise, some quick thinking on Chester's part, and a bloody great deal of luck I dare say that our bodies would still be up there now."

"Well, if the Nazis were able to get up there…" the sergeant began, equivocating.

Sibyl silenced him with a glance. "They had men, and equipment, and most importantly the benefit of time. And they enjoyed the luxury of carrying out their operation in relative secrecy without enemy forces hounding them. If the major tasks us with the mission that I suspect he has in mind, we would be ascending into terrain that would be treacherous and deadly on its own, and difficult enough to survive, without the added risk of marching directly into some sort of well-fortified enemy stronghold!"

Sibyl was more worked up than Jun could remember seeing her before. The Englishwoman's cheeks flushed red and a vein stood out on the side of her forehead, eyes flashing as she spoke. Jun couldn't help but wonder whether something about the topic had touched a nerve. Normally

Sibyl's anecdotes about her late husband or the many quotations and sayings that she attributed to him brought a smile to the Englishwoman's face, as if the mere act of remembering the man brought other happy memories along in its wake. But perhaps there was something about the recollection of this mountain climbing expedition the two had taken part in before the war that was different?

Before Jun could chime in to inquire or the sergeant had the chance to mount some sort of reply, Werner came back from the sink, toweling the last flecks of shaving cream from his now clean-shaven chin.

"Frau Beaton is once again correct, Sergeant," the German soldier said in a calm, level tone. He nodded in Sibyl's direction, who scowled and refused to meet his gaze. "Whatever it is that the major intends, if it involves us scaling an Alpine peak then I fear that our chances of survival are perilously slim, and our chances of successfully completing our mission objectives are even less likely."

Curtis was now sitting on the edge of his bunk with his shoulders slumped and his head in his hands, groaning audibly. "Look, forget I even said anything, all right? I mean, at this point we don't even really know *what* the mission brief is, do we? I'm the last one to walk on the sunny side of the street and try to find the silver lining in every storm cloud, but maybe we should at least wait and hear what the major has in mind before we start wailing and pulling out our hair by the roots?"

The sergeant turned to the young American with one eyebrow raised, a bemused expression on his face.

"I didn't know better," Josiah said, "I'd've said that you were quoting our Mrs. Beaton there, son. That sounded almost like optimism."

Curtis groaned even louder as he pushed off the bunk and onto his feet, and began staggering towards the sinks at the rear of the barracks to clean up. "Just let me finish waking up before we go get the bad news, willya?"

"Hurry up, then," the sergeant said, standing up. He reached down to pick up his pack, and Jun caught a brief wince of pain flash across the sergeant's face as he shifted his weight. Then Josiah straightened up suddenly, back arched and shoulders pushed together, as he pushed the palm of one hand into the small of his back, gritting his teeth.

"Is everything all right, sergeant?" Jun asked, genuinely concerned.

"Y-yeah," Sergeant Josiah answered, his voice choked. "Maybe slept on one of those rocks myself, huh?"

Jun wasn't convinced. Her father had complained about back pains in his later years, and she had seen him struggling with the odd pulled muscle or joint pain when standing or shifting position suddenly. Her father had said it was just the price of getting to live to old age, existing in a body long enough that eventually parts of it begin no longer to function properly.

"My dad used to throw out his back like that," Jun said, stepping closer to the still grimacing sergeant. "He always said it was common as we get older. I used to be able to help past it by pulling his shoulders and…"

Josiah danced out of Jun's reach just as she was getting closer.

"Who said anything about getting 'older,' now?" the sergeant said, still wincing but with an annoyed look on his face and an angry tone to his words. "Just twisted a little strange, that's all. I'm not *old*."

"Of course not," Jun hastened to reply. She knew that the sergeant was always cagey about his age, but that he was clearly older than he usually let on. It was seldom discussed, but he did tend to get defensive whenever the suggestion arose that the years might have taken their toll. "Here, let me."

Jun reached down and grabbed hold of the strap of the sergeant's backpack, then lifted it and held it out towards him. It was somewhat heavier than her own pack, but not by much, and it wasn't a particular strain to hold up at arms' length.

"I've got it, okay?" the sergeant said through gritted teeth, still sounding somewhat annoyed but clearly making an effort to restrain himself. He slung the backpack over one shoulder, jaw clenched and shoulders hunched up as he tried to mask any sign of discomfort that he might be experiencing. "Now get your own gear together, we need to move out."

"Yes, sir," Jun said, resisting the urge to snap off a salute, and hurried back to her bunk to finish packing up her things. She glanced around the barracks at the rest of the squad as she did so. Tempers that might otherwise have flared had cooled, and the discussions of the morning had failed to erupt into full-blown disagreements. At times such as this she felt a kind of kinship to these four people who had been complete strangers to her only a few short months before. The weeks and months that they had spent side-by-side since then—the hardships they had endured together and the dangers they had faced as a team—had knitted them together as close as any family. Whatever perils might lay in store for them, whatever impossible task might be set before them to complete, she knew at least that she could count on each and every member of the squad to have her back, and she trusted that each of them knew that they could count on her as well. Men and women brought together from the four corners of the world, to fight as one to protect the living from the armies of the Dead...

"God damn it," Curtis shouted from the sinks at the rear of the barracks, "which one of you jokers used up all the damn hot water?!"

Jun shook her head. She just hoped that they would all survive the days to come...

CHAPTER 12

"FIRST AND FOREMOST," Major Wilkins said as he began the mission briefing, a broad smile stretching beneath his bushy mustache, "don't for a moment imagine that I'm ordering you simply to march up the side of a mountain."

Curtis Goodwin turned to Jun and the rest of the squad with a smug expression on his face, and silently mouthed, "See, I *told* you" to them all.

"The mere idea is preposterous," the major went on. "That would take far too long, and time is of the essence."

Jun watched as Curtis's smug expression melted into a look of crushing disappointment and bewildered confusion. She stifled a giggle behind her hand, turning her attention back to the major.

"Well, if you don't mind me asking…?" Sergeant Josiah began.

"Of course, of course," the major answered,

waving a hand dismissively, "always happy to hear comments and suggestions from the rank and file, my door is always open, that sort of thing. Never let it be said that Colin Alistair Wilkins is a stickler for needless hierarchy and hidebound tradition, blind to the possibilities inherent in questioning accepted wisdom, eh? No, I should say not. I dare say that none of us would be here today if we had failed to adapt in the early days of the Dead War, what? Survival is the name of the game, and adaptation is key to survival. How does that bit from Darwin go, survival of the fitted?"

"Fittest, sir," corrected the man with the neatly-trimmed mustache wearing a flight suit in the corner of the room, not looking up from the clipboard he was reading. "The core concept of Darwinian evolution can best be expressed as 'survival of the fittest,' though the phrase originates not with Darwin himself but with Herbert Spencer in response to reading the former's 'On The Origin Of The Species', though Darwin later adopted it for his own use in subsequent volumes."

"Quite right," the major plowed ahead after a cursory nod in his direction. "Now, as I was saying, time here is of the essence, and so a more expedient means of getting your team into position will be—"

"Sir?" the sergeant interrupted with a little more urgency to his tone, holding up his hand like a student in a classroom to catch the major's attention.

"What is it now, man?" Major Wilkins replied, blustering.

"I never actually asked my question, is all." Sergeant Josiah was clearly trying to keep his tone respectful, but Jun could see that he was struggling a bit with it.

"Well, get on with it, then." The major leaned back, crossing his arms over his chest, a slight scowl on his face. Then, before the sergeant had even had a chance to reply, the major gestured impatiently and added, "Come along, we haven't got all day. Time being of the essence, as I said…?"

"How," Josiah began, keeping his tone even tempered, "are we supposed to get up the mountain?" He paused, and then added with emphasis, "Sir?"

"I was getting to that, confound it," Major Wilkins snarled back. "If you hadn't been distracting me with talk about evolution and such like I'd have already gone over that by now."

Curtis leaned in close to Jun's side and in a voice scarcely above a whisper said, "We are all going to die."

"Now where was I?" the major went on, thankfully not having heard the young American's words.

"Something about Darwin, dear?" Sibyl chimed in, sweetly.

"No, dash it all," the major scowled, "now I've lost the thread…"

"Post hoc ergo propter hoc," the man in the flight-suit in the corner said, his eyes still on the clipboard in his hands. He flipped over the top page and studied the one beneath just as closely.

"What's that, Hector?" Major Wilkins said, glancing over in the man's direction. Jun recognized him from the mess tent the night before, the one who had been reading a stack of letters and laughing. He didn't seem to be finding his clipboard this morning as entertaining, but it evidently was equally as engrossing. He had barely looked up from it since Jun and the rest of the squad had entered the room. "What's that gibberish you were spouting, now?"

"It was Latin, sir, but it is not really germane." He lowered the clipboard and fixed his gaze on the major. "I believe you were about to introduce my role in the proceedings, unless I am very much mistaken."

The major looked momentarily confused, and

in response the man named Hector held his hands out at shoulder height, swaying back and forth slightly as he made a humming sound that faintly resembled the airplane engines that had roused Jun from slumber that morning.

"Ah, yes, a capital suggestion." The major clapped his hands in triumph, and then gestured in Hector's direction as he turned his attention back to the sergeant and the rest of the squad. "Allow me to present Captain Hector Jennings, late of the RAF, seconded to the Resistance at the beginning of the current difficulties. You could not be in safer hands."

And with that, Major Wilkins simply turned on his heel and marched out of the room.

Jun caught the sergeant's eye, and could see that he was as perplexed by the major's sudden departure as she was.

"You'll have to excuse the major," Hector said as he stepped in front of the squad, both hands on the clipboard held at waist-height. "He's a decent chap and a ruddy good leader when the chips are down, but it all takes its toll on him and he can get a bit dotty when the pressure is off. Still, acta non verba, eh?"

"He seemed lucid enough over dinner last night," Sibyl observed, looking towards the door through which the major had just exited. "A trifle maudlin, perhaps, but otherwise right as rain."

"Oh, don't get me wrong, the old boy isn't quite clapped out just yet. He's still right enough in the head. But with all of those poor souls gone for six after the bally rotters made it over the wall...? It weighs heavily on him, is all I'm saying, and sometimes gets a touch preoccupied." Hector drummed his fingers on the clipboard and chewed the corners of his mustache. Then he shrugged and put a smile on his face. "Still, ad meliora, eh, what?"

Hector paused expectantly, as if waiting for some kind of response, but Jun and the others just treated him to blank stares.

"Ad meliora?" he repeated, like a teacher prompting a classroom with a hint and waiting for one of the students to come up with the correct answer. Then he translated, sighing, "Towards better things, then?"

"You've got our full attention, cap'n." Sergeant Josiah crossed his arms over his chest and sighed. "Lead on, Macduff."

Hector brightened immediately, eyes widening.

"Ah, another devotee of the bard, I see," he said eagerly. "Though as I'm sure you know, the original line was actually 'lay on, Macduff,' and Macbeth was in fact exhorting his Macduff to carry out a vigorous attack upon himself rather than to lead him anywhere, though the line has been commonly misquoted and misapplied since the middle of the last century when…"

The sergeant cleared his throat loudly, interrupting the captain's ramble.

"The briefing?" Josiah said pointedly, remaining immobile with his arms still crossed. "I seem to recall there was some suggestion that you might explain how it is we're expected to reach the top of a danged mountain?"

Hector blinked several times, mouth hanging open slightly, as if caught unawares and needing a moment to process what he'd heard.

"Oh, I'd thought that much was obvious," he finally said with an amused chuckle. "I'll be escorting you there myself."

By way of illustration, as he'd done a short while before, Hector held his hands at shoulder height and swayed slightly back and forth.

"In an airplane," he added, speaking loudly and over-enunciating as if addressing the hard of hearing or the dimwitted.

Jun and the others exchanged a glance.

"You expect to land a plane on top of a goddamn mountain?" Curtis said in disbelief, more or less speaking for them all.

"Oh, good heavens, no," Hector answered hurriedly, shaking his head. "I'm a dab hand behind the stick, I'll be the first to admit, but even I wouldn't try to set a kite down on those rocky peaks. Quickest way to get the chop I can think of. It'd be a damned short flight and no return trip for any of us. No, we'll be hedge-hopping it as low as possible to reduce our exposure to any flack, and the second you lot join the Caterpillar Club I'll jink away and back up into the wild blue yonder, as the Yanks call it."

Jun was still trying to work out what "gone for six" meant exactly, and was having increasing difficulty following everything that Hector was saying. She'd prided herself on picking up British and American idioms fairly quickly on arriving at Woolwich late the previous year, having found that the more formal English that she'd learned in the course of her duties as a diplomat's attaché only somewhat resembled the language as actually used by native speakers. But listening to Captain Jennings speak reminded her of those first nights after she'd arrived in the barracks for anti-necro training, where she could identify almost every word spoken to her but often struggled to interpret the speaker's actual meaning.

But glancing over at her squad mates, Jun could

see that she was far from the only one who was struggling to follow what Hector was saying.

"Caterpillar... Club?" Curtis was the first to give voice to the confusion that Jun was sure that they all shared.

"Sure, caterpillar as in 'silk,' eh, what? Umbrellas?" Hector grinned for a moment, then the grin began to fade as he saw the bewildered looks that persisted on the faces of the squad. "Silk as in parachutes?"

Jun could hear Sibyl gasp, and thought that the Englishwoman might be frightened, but when she glanced in her direction Jun could see a smile playing at the corners of Sibyl's mouth as her eyes flashed, and she knew that had been a gasp of excitement and not one of fear. From the stories she told of her adventures before the war, Sibyl had made it clear that she had been a thrill seeker in her younger days, and the thought of jumping out of an airplane was obviously appealing to her.

For her part, Jun was less certain.

"You *have* all been trained up on parachuting, haven't you?" Hector asked, a note of uncertainty creeping into his voice.

Jun and the others alternatively shook their heads or muttered "No" or some combination of the two.

"Well, then," Hector tucked the clipboard under one arm and rubbed his hands together in anticipation. "In that case we should get started. I think the training rig is still set up in the old hangar, assuming we can drag together enough mattresses or bales of hay for you to…"

Whatever Hector had been about to say would have to remain a mystery, as his voice was suddenly drowned out by the piercing peals of alarm bells sounding from somewhere outside the building.

"The devil…? Hector said, turning in the direction of the door.

A heartbeat later, as if in response, the door slammed open and Major Wilkins thrust his head and shoulders inside.

"Don't just stand there with your tongues hanging out!" the major barked, eyes bright and clear, his manner focused and driven. "We've got hostiles on the fence and I need all hands on deck manning the walls. The blighters won't get through a second time, or on all of our heads be it!"

The somewhat scattered major who had left the room only a short time before had been immediately transformed by the sudden emergence of a threat, it seemed, the encroaching danger sharpening his thoughts and wits to a razor's edge.

"You heard the man," Sergeant Josiah said,

racing over to where his Springfield M1903 lay propped against the wall. "We've got a job to do."

Hector, who seemed completely in charge when discussing all matters aviation-related, had instantly ceded authority to Josiah the moment that a terrestrial-bound threat presented itself. Without question or comment and without missing a beat, the pilot drew his Enfield No. 2 revolver from the holster at his hip and fell in line with the rest of the squad as they followed the sergeant racing through the door and out of the room.

"I shouldn't worry, miss," Hector said to Jun with a smile as they filed out side by side. "We'll soon have this bother sorted out and have you parachuting in no time!"

For the first time Jun found herself grateful for an unexpected zombie attack. Anything that delayed the moment when she would have to strap on a parachute and jump out of a plane was a welcome distraction at this point, even a horde of flesh-hungry undead. At least she could face the Dead with her feet planted firmly on the ground.

CHAPTER 13

As SHE STOOD atop the wall that encircled the base camp, peering through the telescopic sights of her T-99 at the Dead horde massing below, Jun found herself regretting her choice of words only moments before. Because while she was not yet being forced to leap from a plane, neither was she able to face the present danger with the ground beneath her feet. Instead she was perched awkwardly on a narrow ledge that ran along the inner side of the stockade fence, with only a low railing between her and the open air behind her. Even as relatively short as she was, it would be a matter of ease for her to step over the railing if she choose to do so; and while stepping over the railing into the empty air beyond was the last thing on her mind, still she worried that it would be all too easy to accidentally topple over it if she weren't careful, with a long fall to the hard ground below.

The winds were picking up, not only carrying with them the scent of putrefaction and decay from the approach horde of the Dead, but also serving to buffet Jun and knock her off balance. With her right hand over her T-99's trigger and her left hand steadying its stock, she couldn't reach out and take hold of the top of the stockade fence to steady herself, and instead had to continually shift her weight from one leg to the other, constantly moving her center of gravity to maintain her position. It made sighting for targets more difficult than normal, which only complicated what were already trying circumstances.

Jun had originally assumed that it had been the arrival of a new group of undead shamblers that had occasioned the ringing of the base camp's alarm bells, but when she and the rest of her squad had first climbed to the top of the ramparts she had been surprised to see that there were only a handful of zombies shuffling about along the northern edge of the electrified perimeter fence that ran all around the camp, with a handful more approaching from the north. The heightened response seemed disproportionate to the threat, and caused Jun to wonder whether Major Wilkins's unsettled thoughts and feelings of guilt about the recent undead incursion into the camp had lead him to overreact. The major would not be the first combatant in the Dead War driven to make irrational decisions by undigested fears from a previous fight, even one that he had himself survived unharmed.

But then Sergeant Josiah had drawn her attention to the fallen log draped over the wire at the northwest corner of the perimeter fence, and suddenly Jun had a better understanding of the urgency of the situation.

"I'm telling you, it's just a coincidence!" Curtis shouted as he fired a round from his M1 Carbine at one of the zombies that was shuffling towards the base of the stockade fence. Another of the Dead was in the process of clambering over the log that lay across the wire fence some distance behind. "It's not like these jokers can strategize."

"You put a considerable amount of faith in the likelihood of the most unlikely of coincidence, dear boy," Sibyl answered out of the corner of her mouth, taking a pot shot at the Dead who was just now stepping off the fallen log and onto the no-man's land between the outer wire fence and the inner wooden stockade. "Isn't it easier to accept that they knocked it down on *purpose*?"

Whether by accident or by design, it had become immediately apparent to Jun and the rest of the squad that the approaching group of zombies had collided with one of the dead trees that stood a short distance away from the outer perimeter fence, and that the collision had caused a limb that had clearly already been close to dropping to fall to the ground. And again, either through intention or happenstance, the log had fallen directly onto the electrified wire fence, one end resting on the ground outside the fence, the other hanging a few feet in the air above the ground within. The wire fence was sturdily built enough that it had withstood the added strain, though the metal posts on either side were bowed inwards somewhat by the additional weight. And though a strong electrical current still flowed through the wire, the wood that made up the fallen log was apparently dry enough that it was not especially conductive, as the zombies that crawled up and over the log did not suffer the same ill effects from electrocution that the undead who grappled other parts of the fence were currently displaying.

Effectively, the zombies had managed to create a makeshift bridge that allowed them to circumvent the electrified fence, and could now reach the inner fence directly. There were few enough of them that the snipers atop the ramparts were able to keep them from climbing to the top, but enough that the danger they posed was still very real.

For her part, Jun felt that the fact that some of the zombies were still trying to climb directly over the metal wire at other points along the perimeter fence argued strongly in favor of the notion that the whole thing had been happenstance and not strategy. The smell of cooking flesh was strong in her nostrils.

"There's more of the blighters approaching from the east!" Major Wilkins called out from a few dozen feet to Jun's right.

She glanced in the direction that the major was pointing, and saw another horde of the Dead advancing on their position through a stand of trees. If they continued to advance in roughly the same trajectory then their path would carry them right towards the fallen log that breeched the perimeter, and then the squad would have even more of the undead to contend with on the inner side of the electrified fence.

"Someone has to clear that damned fence," Jun heard the sergeant swear beneath his breath at her side.

As if in response, though Jun was sure that there was no way that the major could have heard him, Major Wilkins shouted down the line in their direction.

"Sergeant, take another member of your squad to assist you and get out there and get that bloody log off of my bloody fence!"

Sergeant Josiah just nodded in the major's direction, then turned towards the ladder which lead back to the ground.

"You're with me, kid," he said as he rushed past Jun, slinging his Springfield across his back as he went. Then he called back to the rest of the squad, "The rest of y'all, keep the bastards off our backs while we work, you hear?"

As Jun moved towards the ladder after him, Hector moved out of line to follow close behind her.

"I'll join you if you don't mind," Hector called down to the sergeant who was already approaching the main gate in the stockade fence. He waggled the Enfield No. 1 revolver that he held in one hand. "I'm not much good with this peashooter of mine at long range, but I'm a sure enough shot that I should be able to help keep the rotters off your back from close up. Press on regardless, eh?"

"The more the merrier," Josiah answered with a humorless grin as took hold of his 12-gauge shotgun with one hand and rested his other on the handle that would open the main gate. "Y'all ready to hustle?"

Jun and Hector nodded in reply, readying their weapons.

"Okay, then, on three…" Josiah tightened his grip on his shotgun, his jaw clenched in concentration.

"I'll get that!" One of the junior officers who had been manning the wall when the squad arrived the night before was hurrying over, waving his arms to get the sergeant's attention. He skidded to a halt just short of the door and gestured towards the handle. "The major says I'm to let you out and then keep the gate shut until you've got the foreground cleared."

Josiah tilted his head to one side, and only slowly took his hand away from the handle. "Sounds to me like could be the major isn't so sure we'll be coming back in at all…"

The officer just shrugged, and took hold of the handle himself. "You shout out and I'll get the bloody thing opened quick as a wink, you've got my word on it."

Josiah didn't reply, but readied to fire his shotgun, and then stood in position while Jun and Hector moved into place on either side of him. Then he nodded towards the junior officer, raised the stock of his shotgun to his shoulder, and narrowed his eyes.

From atop the stockade fence the barrage of fire

from their squad mates and the other defenders of the camp intensified.

"Let's go, already!" the sergeant shouted, and in response the junior officer yanked down on the handle and the gate swung open.

The rotting remains of the fallen undead already littered the ground beyond the stockade fence, and as Jun and the others advanced through the gate into the zone marked out by the wooden fence within and the electrified wire without, there were still more of the zombies lurching towards them. From where Jun stood, she could see even more scrambling over the log across the wire fence.

Jun swung up the barrel of her Thompson submachine gun, but before she was able to squeeze the trigger and fire, the head of the zombie that she was targeting exploded.

"We'll keep the flies away, dear," the voice of Sibyl called down from the ramparts above. "You stem the tide and keep more from getting in!"

As if to punctuate her words, the Englishwoman potted another round with her Lee Enfield at one of the shambling Dead who was lurching towards Jun with its arms outstretched and bony hands grasping. Sibyl's shot hit true, and a bloom of black ichor blossomed on the forehead of the sunken-cheeked wretch a split second before the back of its skull blew out and rotted brains and bone fragments sprayed out over the heads and shoulders of the zombies bringing up the rear.

"Come on, then!" the sergeant roared as he fired first one round and then another from his pump-action shotgun, hitting two of the Dead in rapid succession, sending both of their lifeless corpses sprawling to the ground like marionettes whose strings had both been cut in one fell swoop.

Jun and Hector followed close behind Josiah as he advanced steadily to the northeastern corner of the enclosure, where the fallen limb traversed the perimeter fence.

Though there were still only a relatively few of the zombies within the fence, they were packed so closely together that it was difficult to draw a bead on any one of them individually. Waving arms and the erratic shambling of the Dead in the lead tended to draw the fire of the defenders along the wall drawing their sights on the Dead bringing up the rear, so that despite a constant barrage of sniper fire from atop the stockade fence, still Jun and her two companions found that they were advancing towards a small horde of the Dead who remained on their feet, defiantly upright and blocking their path towards the fallen log.

Suddenly and without warning, one of the faster-moving zombies burst from the pack, and it took Jun only a split second to see the primed grenade clutched against its bony chest.

Only bare seconds remained before the suicide zombie closed the ground that separated them. Jun raised her Thompson but managed to squeeze the trigger a split-second too soon, so that the submachine gun burst hit the suicide zombie not in the head as she'd intended but full in its abdomen. And though the burst blew large chunks away from the zombie's rotting torso that flew away and fell to the ground some distance away with a sickening sound, the shot did nothing to halt the zombie's forward motion.

The zombie was only steps away now. Jun raised the barrel of her submachine gun but had trouble drawing a bead. She needed to make the next shot count or else...

Between one heartbeat and the next, Hector charged forward directly into the path of the oncoming suicide zombie. With his left hand he took hold of the grenade, and he used his right to drive the barrel of his Enfield No. 2 directly up under the zombie's lower jaw. Hector wrenched the grenade free from the zombie's grip at the same instant that he fired a round from his revolver directly up and through the zombie's rotting brain.

And then without hesitating an instant, he reversed and hurled the grenade away from himself as far and as hard as possible.

The grenade detonated in midair directly above the horde of Dead who crowded together on the far side of the electrified fence. The shrapnel rained down on them, driving into the heads and hearts of more than a few of the Dead, dropping them to the ground.

"Well *done*!" Jun could not help exclaiming, sincerely impressed. Not only had his quick thinking potentially saved her life, but he appeared to have given them the breathing room they needed to get the job done.

"Yes, yes, I hit for a six, but there'll be time for pats on the back when we're through," Hector shot back without turning around. "Now get weaving before we touch bottom!"

Jun wasn't sure the precise meaning of Hector's words but the general sense was clear enough. They needed to make use of every advantage they had.

With the stem of Dead coming over the traversing log temporarily slowed by Hector's well-placed grenade toss, they only had to clear the zombies who still stood in their way and then they could shove the offending limb off the wire fence before any more of them made it over. Sibyl and the others atop the rampart were still busily picking off the Dead who had broken from the pack and advanced towards the stockade fence, so only a handful remained between the sergeant's ad hoc fireteam and their goal.

"Run and gun, serpentine!" Sergeant Josiah called back over his shoulder as he charged forward, hitting another of the Dead square in the face with a blast from his 12-gauge, then jinking to one side before pumping another round in the chamber and firing again and haring off in a slightly different direction. "Don't give them time to close with you!"

They were getting closer to the electrical fence by the moment, but every instant that passed meant that more of the undead were approaching the perimeter from the east, and the greater the chances that one of the shamblers milling around the edge of the wire fence would make it up and over the log.

Hector blasted one of the Dead in the face with his revolver just as Jun picked off another with a short burst from her submachine gun, and suddenly they were within arm's reach of the fallen limb.

"You keep them bastards at bay, kid," the sergeant ordered, slinging his shotgun over his shoulder. "Captain, help me get this damned thing off of here."

Jun nodded a silent assent, and took up her position just to one side of the breech as Josiah and Hector each took a hold of the log and tried to push it up and over the fence.

There were a handful of Dead still up and walking in the zone between the perimeter and the stockade, and while most of them still seemed intent on scaling the wooden fence, no doubt drawn by the life and heat of those within, one or two of them had taken notice of Jun and her companions, and were redirecting their steps to carry them back towards the electrified fence and the more readily available prey standing there.

"We got more trying to get over!" Josiah shouted.

Glancing back Jun could see another of the shamblers trying to climb up on the fallen limb from the other side. She fired a round at the nearest of the Dead approaching her from the stockade, then turned and fired at the shambler on the outside of the perimeter who was just now mounting the fallen limb. Her first shot hit a little wide, blasting a hole in the zombie's shoulder but doing little to arrest its forward progress. The zombie had gotten on top of the fallen log with both feet squarely under it before Jun's second shot hit it dead center in its forehead. The zombie toppled, but instead of falling on the outside of the perimeter, its headless corpse landed so that it was draped over the top wire of the perimeter fence, and began popping and smoldering as electrical current surged through its lifeless form.

"Any time now, sir," Jun urged as she turned back around to fire at another of the approaching Dead from the inner zone of the perimeter, then swung back to scan for any others attempting to climb over the fallen log.

"Trying!" Josiah shouted back. "Damn thing won't budge!"

"It seems to be snagged on the wire," Hector observed, bending down to look sidelong at the place where the irregular bark and broken branches on the fallen limb touched the perimeter fence itself.

"Careful not to touch it!" Josiah cautioned. "If you as much as brush against that wire, then ZAP, you're done for."

"I've worked with electrical systems since the first day of flight school, sir," Hector answered, a little haughtily, "so I like to think that I know how to handle myself around a livewire…"

Sparks arced between the top and middle wires of the perimeter fence, causing Hector to jump back, eyes wide with alarm.

"Point taken," he said quietly, with evident relief.

"We've got more incoming," Jun said as she fired a short burst at another zombie who was close to mounting the fallen lob on the other side of the fence.

Josiah and Hector were wrenching the log back and forth as hard as they could, causing the wires to thrum like guitar strings as they did, but still the fallen limb seemed bound to the wires of the fence as if welded to them.

"Maybe if we set fire to the damned thing?" Josiah said through gritted teeth as he wrestled with the end of the fallen limb.

"Wouldn't that muck with the electricity?" Hector looked puzzled.

"How should I know?" the sergeant snarled. "I thought you were the expert in electrics!"

Now the defenders atop the ramparts, having dispatched all of the Dead who had made it over the log and into the inner zone, were directing their fire at the zombies approaching from outside the perimeter fence. For a brief moment, at least, Jun could turn her attention away from the Dead on the other side of the fence, with Sibyl and the others covering the approaches.

"Let me help," she said, slinging her Thompson

M1A1 onto her back and putting her shoulder to the log.

"Okay, on three," the sergeant said, pressing both hands against the underside of the fallen limb and nodding to Hector to slide into position on the opposite side of Jun. "One. Two. *Push*!"

Jun clenched her jaw with the strain of shoving up on the end of the log, and the top wire of the electrified fence hummed like a harp string with the reverberations of their efforts. They pushed with all of their might, straining to the breaking point, but still the wood remained stubbornly hooked onto the wire itself.

The trio slowly eased off, catching their breath after the exertion.

"Well, maybe we should try burning the bally thing, at that?" Hector said, panting.

Jun reached up a hand and felt the outer layer of bark on the end of the log. She was able to flake off a section of the bark with her fingertip, revealing the dried wood below. An idea was slowly coming into focus in her head.

"Hang on, let me try something," she said, and motioned for Josiah and Hector to step back. Then she unslung the Thompson from her back, took aim at the branch itself a few inches away from the point where it traversed the wire fence, and then emptied the remainder of her drum magazine into the wood, spraying machinegun fire in a narrow arc from the top of the branch to the bottom and back again.

As she was pulling the emptied drum off the Thompson and reaching for a refill, Josiah stepped forward and put a hand on her shoulder. "I think I see what you've got in mind, let me give it a shot."

Jun stepped aside as the sergeant moved into position, and emptied round after round from his pump-action shotgun into the branch in the same spot that Jun had targeted. Splinters and bits of shattered bark flew in all directions. The log remained in one piece, but daylight was breaking through in tiny places here and there.

When the sergeant's shotgun ran dry, Jun stepped forward and grabbed hold of the end of the branch once more. "Now, don't push *up*," she said, glancing back over her shoulder at the sergeant and Hector who were both taking up their positions on either side of her, "pull *down*."

The three of them put their full weight into it, Jun so much so that at one point her feet were lifted off the ground as she dangled full body from the end of the limb. And at first it appeared that they were having no better luck this time than any of their earlier attempts, but then a series of loud cracks and pops could be heard, one right after another. More splinters were flying from the limb now, as the wood began to bend along the seam etched out by their barrage of gunfire. Like perforations in a piece of card, the holes that their bullets and shot had driven through the limb had weakened the wood just enough to make a difference.

For a moment Jun worried that the added weight and strain they were putting on the fence might snap the wires from their moorings on the posts, but the major's crews had clearly built to last. With a final sigh, the portion of the limb overhanging the inner side of the fence broke free in their hands, with the fence's wires still holding fast.

"Damn it!" Josiah spat as Jun and Hector threw the severed limb to one side. "God *damn* it!"

Jun could see immediately what the sergeant was reacting to. While they had succeeded in breaking off the part of the limb that overhung the fence, the other half of the fallen log was still propped up against the fence's top wire. The Dead still had their ramp up and over the fence, provided they maintained their balance and didn't hit the electrified wire before getting across.

Or so it appeared.

"Look out!" Jun said, raising the barrel of her Thompson and aiming at the far side of the fence.

The jostling horde of undead had been joined by the newcomers that they had seen approaching from the east, and even with the relentless barrage of sniper fire from atop the ramparts, one or two of the Dead had succeeded in reaching the spot where the end of the fallen limb met the ground.

Jun hit one of the encroaching zombies squarely in the face with a short burst, sending it staggering back as the back of its head exploded. But another of the zombies was already clambering onto the makeshift ramp.

Hector was already firing off rounds from his Enfield revolver as Jun swung the barrel of her submachine gun up and sighted for the zombie's head, but suddenly and without warning the log slipped off the top wire and slammed hard onto the ground on the far side of the fence. The force of their attempts to dislodge the limb, or the loss of the overhanging portion, or a combination of the two, had apparently dislodged whatever part of the log had been snagged on the wire, so that the weight of the zombie trying to climb over had been enough to pull it loose and send it crashing down to earth.

For the briefest of instants the top wire oscillated widely up and down, like a guitar string violently strummed. But the zombie who had been attempting to climb over the log when it fell was pitching forward, skeletal arms flailing. It sprawled across the top wire of the fence and immediately began twitching violently as the strong electrical current surged through its rotting flesh. The inhuman shriek the Dead had made as it was being electrocuted still echoed in Jun's ears as the stench of its charring flesh reached her nostrils.

CHAPTER 14

"WELL, THAT WORKED, I guess," Josiah said, shrugging slowly as he wrinkled his nose in distaste. He and Hector had picked up the broken half of the wooden branch, and used it to push the electrocuted zombies off of the perimeter fence and sent their rotting corpses flopping down to the ground beyond.

"Good show!" came a voice shouting from behind them, and turning around Jun could see Major Wilkins shouting down from the ramparts above. He was motioning broadly with his arm, waving towards the gate in the stockade fence. "Get back inside, and quickly now!"

Hector clearly didn't need to be told twice, and took off jogging back towards the gate right away. But Jun was a firm believer in hierarchies and the chain of command, and turned to Josiah to get direction.

"You heard the man, kid," the sergeant said, nodding towards the gate. "We did the job, now let's get out of here before anything else starts dropping out of the sky on us."

As Jun and the sergeant raced back to the gate that was already cranking open to allow them in, she couldn't help but moan. In all of the commotion and confusion of the preceding minutes that they'd spent clearing the inner zone of the Dead and removing the breech from the fence, she hadn't had the chance to give a moment's thought to their impending mission, but the sergeant's statement about things falling out of the sky brought it rushing back to her.

Just as the ground would soon be rushing up towards her, Jun thought, and suppressed a shudder.

A SHORT WHILE later, pulling straw out of her hair and struggling to catch her breath, Jun revised her earlier opinion somewhat. Jumping out of a plane wasn't just terrifying. It was also really, really annoying.

Or at least, attempting to learn the skills involved had proved to be so.

"A good attempt," Hector was saying, his tone more cheery and encouraging that the bruises on Jun's arms and legs seemed to merit, "but you need to bend those legs and roll when you hit or you'll have trouble walking away. Now back up the ladder and give it another shot, the lot of you."

They were in a wooden structure that had been a barn for a family farm before the Dead War and the mass evacuation of the region. When the Resistance had set up their basecamp in the area, they had converted the farm's fields into a makeshift runway for the small fleet of aircraft that flew in and out of the camp, and used the barn as a sort of hangar. At the rear of the structure there was a platform high overhead that had once been a hayloft, and after the Vickers Wellington twin-engine bomber that had been housed in the hangar was pushed out onto the runway for servicing by a small ground crew, parachuting rigging had been strung up from the rafters above a collection of hay bales and mattresses that were arranged on the floor.

For the last hour, ever since they had come back inside the stockade after clearing the breech in the perimeter fence, Jun and the others had been climbing a ladder up onto the platform, strapping themselves into the parachute harnesses, and then following Hector's step-by-step instructions as they approached the edge of the platform, got into the correct positions, and then jumped down onto the pile of hay bales and mattresses below.

Hector's instructions had focused on three main areas: how to properly strap into the harnesses, how and when to pull the ripcord after jumping out of the plane, and how to arrange their bodies to lessen the impact of landing as much as possible. So far, Jun and the others had managed to grasp the essentials of getting into the harnesses in short order, and were beginning to get a better sense of how to manage the ripcord, but as to hitting the ground? The learning curve was a steep one and they still had a considerable amount of climbing left to do.

Or falling, Jun thought, as the case may be.

The five members of the squad had reached the top of the ladder and the sergeant was in the process of strapping into the practice harness when from outside they could hear a sound like distant thunder, steady and unbroken and gradually growing louder.

On the floor below the platform, Hector brightened and clapped his hands together once, smiling in anticipation.

"Let's break there, chaps!" he called up to the squad.

The sound like distant thunder was growing even louder, and was joined by another thrum coming along behind, quiet at first but growing louder by the moment.

"Bang on the dot," Hector said with a glance at his wristwatch. He had turned and was walking towards the open doors of the barn/hangar.

Josiah was shrugging out of the practice harness with a slightly annoyed expression on his face. "We just supposed to wait up here, then?"

"Of course not," Hector called back over his shoulder, cheerily. "You'll want to hear what they have to say, I'm sure."

Jun and the others exchanged a confused glance, then dutifully climbed back down the ladder. At least they wouldn't have to jump the twenty feet to the ground again this time around.

By the time the five of them had all reached the bottom and crossed the floor to the open door, Hector had already made his way out to the edge of the makeshift airfield that ran alongside the rear of the camp. It was a short runway, by necessity, enclosed entirely inside the stockade fence that bisected the former farm fields on either side, and it seemed to Jun that it would take expert flying to take off or land on such a relatively small strip of land.

But whoever was at the sticks of the two Spitfires coming in for landing clearly seemed to be experts, given how gracefully they were approaching the landing zone.

Jun and the others fell into line behind Hector, who was yet again checking over a clipboard as he had been that morning. Jun realized that the planes that were landing must be the same ones whose take-off had woken her that morning. They had to be the dawn patrol returning from their maneuvers.

The first of the Spitfires had already touched down and was taxiing across the makeshift landing strip towards the far end of the enclosure as the second Spitfire made its final approach. As Jun watched, the second of the two was wheels down and well into its deceleration run as it gradually slowed to taxiing speed. It seemed to Jun that there was hardly any margin of error at all, and yet both planes had been brought safely to ground without any apparent difficult at all, seemingly effortless to her untrained eye.

Hector's expert eyes, however, had apparently caught sight of some aspects of the landing where there was room for improvement.

The first of the Spitfires had been brought to a halt on the far end of the field, near the spot where the ground crews had been servicing the Vickers Wellington twin-engine bomber, and the pilot was climbing down out of the cockpit to the ground below. The Spitfire pilot was wearing a flight jacket with a fur-lined collar, goggles, and a long scarf wrapped around his neck and the lower half of his face. As he crossed the makeshift airfield towards the spot where Hector waited with his clipboard, the Spitfire pilot unwound the scarf from around his face, so that instead of covering his mouth and chin it was draped around his neck. With the goggles pushed up on his forehead, the scarf flowing behind him in the midday breeze, and a cocky smile on his face, he looked for all the world like the image of an old-fashioned flying ace from the days of the First World War.

"You're still waiting too long to pull back on the stick, Monty," Hector said, glancing up from his clipboard. "I've warned you about it before. You're going to end up pranging that kite of yours one of these days if you don't keep a better eye on your air speed on final approach."

The Spitfire pilot flashed a rakish grin before responding. "You're just too used to flying that lumbering boat of yours, Hector old boy. You've forgotten just what you can do behind the stick of something with a bit more maneuverability."

The second of the Spitfires had taxied to a stop at the far end of the field, and its pilot was jumping down out of the cockpit. She was dressed a little less flamboyantly than her fellow Spitfire pilots, wearing a leather jacket over a pair of coveralls, googles already pushed up onto her forehead, and an old-fashioned looking leather flight helmet. As she crossed the field towards them, she pulled off the googles and the flight helmet, revealing tight black curls cropped close to the scalp, and grinned broadly, her teeth striking white in contrast to her dark skin.

"Here to give me my daily grades, eh, Captain Hector, sir?" the second Spitfire pilot called over to Hector as she drew near. Jun could hear a playful edge to her words.

"You didn't touch bottom in another one of my birds, Ndidi," Hector replied, "so it's still better than your worst to date."

"One time!" the woman named Ndidi replied in mock outrage, holding an index finger up and wagging it in Hector's face. "One time I come in too hot, and I never hear the end of it."

"Don't take it personally, love," the man called Monty called over to her as he headed in the direction of the mess tent at the center of the camp. "He keeps giving me a hard time about my landings and I haven't cracked up on landing even the once."

Ndidi followed in Monty's footsteps, heading towards the former barn.

"Well?" Hector said impatiently as he trailed along behind the two pilots, gesturing with his clipboard. Jun and the rest of the squad followed him. "Did you find it?"

"Oh, we found it all right," Monty said, glancing back over his shoulder in their direction. "Just where we thought it'd be."

"I am just glad that it is to be *you* who goes back there," Ndidi added, pointing with one long finger in Hector's direction. "Because I would much rather not."

"So," Sergeant Josiah said as he glanced over at Hector, "we getting back to learning how to hurl ourselves outta planes or what?" He jerked a thumb over his shoulder in the direction of the barn where they'd spent the morning training.

Hector didn't answer right away, but kept watching the two Spitfire pilots as they entered the mess tent, shaking his head a little ruefully. He turned and walked in the direction they'd gone, motioning for the sergeant and the rest of the squad to follow him.

"Your parachute training will have to wait, I'm

afraid, but best come along with me," he said, sounding a little weary. "Their debriefing can serve as your part of the briefing for *your* operation, so might as well kill two birds with one stone, eh?"

Jun glanced over at Sergeant Josiah and the rest of the squad as they fell into line and trooped along behind Hector. She wasn't sure who were the birds in that formulation and who the stone, and wasn't at all certain that she wanted to find out.

CHAPTER 15

WHEN THE SQUAD and Hector reached the mess tent, the two pilots had obtained cups of steaming-hot tea and plates of lukewarm hash, and had taken up residence at one of the central tables in the dining area.

"So these are the poor bastards who you're planning to drop down into that muck?" Monty said around a mouthful of food as the squad approached the table, addressing Hector but nodding in the direction of Jun and the others.

"Look here, now," Sergeant Josiah began, bristling somewhat, but Hector held up a hand and motioned for a moment's pause as he hastened to intervene.

"These are those lucky sods, indeed," Hector replied to Monty, then turned towards the squad to explain. "When we got word from Major Wilkins that you lot needed ferrying up into the Alps, I sent

Monty and Ndidi here on a recon flight to scout the area and see whether they could locate this mountaintop fortress you're looking for."

He turned his attention back the two pilots at the table. Monty was still shoveling food from his plate into his mouth like it would evaporate if left sitting too long, but Ndidi had pushed her own plate to one side and was in the process of pulling maps and charts out of zippered pockets in her leather jacket and coveralls, and unfolding and spreading them out on the table in front of them.

"So, what's the verdict, you two?" Hector asked the two pilots, his hands on his hips. "Am I going to have any trouble getting these nice people to their destination in one piece?"

The two Spitfire pilots exchanged a glance before answering.

"It could well be a might tricky," Monty replied, guardedly.

"And it could well be that *you* will find it tricky getting back yourself, eh?" Ndidi added, wagging a finger in Hector's direction.

Hector was rubbing his chin with one hand, looking thoughtful. "Bags of flak, I take it?"

Ndidi shook her head, blinking slowly. "No, I spotted emplacements... many of them, in fact... but we didn't take any fire."

"Did they not spot you?" Hector asked.

"Maybe?" Monty shrugged. "We were hedge-hopping as best we could, keeping the peaks between us and a clear line of sight from the enemy's position as much as possible, but that was part and parcel with the problem, wasn't it? Played silly buggers with my kite's attitude controls and I near as damn it went for a Burton without the bally bastards firing a shot."

Jun could see that Hector wasn't catching their precise meaning, and didn't feel so bad that it was entirely escaping her as well. She could see that the other members of her squad were similarly struggling to parse his meaning.

"Can we have that again," Curtis chimed in, "in English this time?"

Monty sighed and shook his head.

"Crosswinds, right?" Monty held his arms up crossed at the wrists in the shape of an X. "With air as thin as it is up there you think it'd be only fair if the winds took it a little easy on you, right? But no, it played holy hell with us as we tried to get through those narrow passes."

"And if you put some angels between you and the ground…?" Hector began.

Jun and Sibyl met each other's gaze, and the Englishwoman mouthed "Angels?" silently in reply to Jun's wordless shrug.

Ndidi shook her head, taking a sip of tea before answering. "Less turbulence at higher altitude, greater danger of flying into the line of enemy fire. As I say, there are a considerable number of defensive emplacements, and those are just the ones I spotted on a few quick passes. Whoever designed that place made certain that it could defend itself easily against an aerial approach."

"But you'll need the higher altitude to give our friends here a chance to get their chutes open," Monty chimed in, scooping up another forkful of hash from his plate. "As it is they'll have a devil of a time putting down exactly where they want to land."

Hector was silent for a long moment, eyes narrowed, deep in thought. Then he leaned forward and rested his hands on the edge of the table, and nodded in the direction of the maps and charts that Ndidi had spread out on the table's surface. "Show me."

Ndidi had a last sip from her cup of tea, and then stood up and moved across the table from Hector, with the map spread between them. She leaned down and pointed to a spot that she'd marked with penciled notations.

"It was right where we thought it would be," she

said, "on the highest peak directly north-northeast of that village identified in the intel provided by those noncombatants we questioned last night. And as far as I was able to determine the rest of their account squares with the facts, as well."

Jun realized that the "noncombatants" Ndidi was talking about must be the refugee villagers that she and the squad had escorted down out of the foothills. And that Major Wilkins must have had the pilots interview them directly after hearing Werner's report the night before. Which only stood to reason, as that way they'd be getting information about the location direct from the primary sources and not filtered through Werner's interrogation of the group en masse out in the ruined village. And now, it appeared that not only had the pilots confirmed the existence of the Alpine Fortress in the first place, but they had reconnoitered its defensive advantages and offensive capacities. Which, granted, had clearly been the pilots' mission objective. Still, Jun couldn't help feeling that as a result the pilots now knew a great deal more about the squad's intended target than Jun or any of the rest of her squadmates did, but as yet the focus of the discussion had centered largely around aerial concerns, with very little about the practical realities of her squad actually carrying out their *own* mission.

Even being a stickler for hierarchy and chain of command as she was, Jun was tempted to give voice to her concern, even though the squad had not been officially invited to provide questions or commentary to what was to all appearances an official debriefing of the two pilots on the part of Hector, their commanding officer. Curtis had already chimed in, of course, but then the young American was hardly one for observing the appropriate chain of command.

But then Jun could breathe easier when Sergeant Josiah stepped forward, arms crossed over his chest and chin jutting forward, and gave voice to exactly the same concerns that were gnawing at her.

"This is all fascinating, I'm sure," Josiah said, "but how about y'all start talking to *us* about just what it is we're jumping into here? What kind of trouble are we looking at, anyway?"

Hector turned to look in the sergeant's direction for a long moment, blinking a few times and looking like he'd lost his place in a prepared statement and struggling to remember what to say next. Then he shook his head abruptly, as though knocking the thoughts themselves loose in his cranium, and gave the sergeant a wan smile.

"Too right, sorry about that, friends," Hector

replied apologetically. "It's one of the immutable laws of aviation: put two pilots in close proximity and we'll talk shop with the same speed and in the same direction until operated on by an unbalanced force. Like conversational inertia, eh?"

Hector paused as if giving time for his listeners to laugh, but when his quip failed to generate so much as a faint chuckle he turned back to Ndidi and Monty and gestured for them to continue.

"Go on, then," Hector said, "just what are we looking at with this so-called Fortress, anti-aircraft defenses aside?"

"It comes by the name, honestly, I can give that much with confidence," Monty replied. "I went in thinking that maybe we'd find some sort of bunker or even just a tarted-up chalet, but no… 'Fortress' fits the bill perfectly. It's like a bloody great castle plopped right on the top of a mountain range."

Ndidi had pulled a stub of a pencil out of an inner pocket of her jacket, and after grabbing one of the charts that she had spread on the table she flipped it over and started sketching on the back.

"It looks to be at least partially built into the side of the mountain itself," Ndidi explained as she continued to sketch out both an elevation of the fortress as seen straight on and a bird's eye view of the layout from above. Though simple and lacking any flourishes, there was sufficient clarity and detail to get the basic ideas across. "There's a small landing pad on the north-west corner of the facility, undoubtedly for helicopters to land, but no indication that there are any on sight."

"So if we had a helicopter we could just land there ourselves?" Curtis said, seeming to brighten at the thought of flying all the way to a landing rather than parachuting from midair. "Pretty thoughtful of them to leave a flat surface waiting for us like that. Might as well have rolled out a welcome mat."

"And I suppose that we should simply knock on the front door and announce our arrival when we do?" Werner replied, curling his lip in distaste. "Or would you presume that they would not notice a helicopter landing on their roof?"

"It's a moot point," Hector interrupted, "because we *don't* have a helicopter, and no way of getting our hands on one in anything like a useful amount of time. But our German friend here is correct. All chance of subtlety, subterfuge, or surprise would be lost if we tried to bring you into a landing under a powered flight. Our only hope is for you to hit silk high enough up and far enough out that under darkness they won't be able to catch a glimpse of you. They might manage to catch sight of the Wellington on their radar scopes if they're quick enough, but my hope is that with Ndidi and Monty here having buzzed them this morning in quick succession, they'd think we were just coming in for another reconnaissance run. At worst it will keep their attention focused on my kite as I fly away and not on any dark specks that might have fallen in my wake."

Ndidi was finishing her sketch of the layout of the fortress as seen from the air, and Jun stepped to her side to get a closer look.

"Sir," Jun said glancing over at Sergeant Josiah, arching an eyebrow. "Permission to speak?"

Josiah sighed dramatically before he answered.

"Kid, you need to stop raising your hand like a kid in a Sunday school class every time you've got something to share. Just spit it out, all ready."

"Sorry, sir," Jun said, gaze dropping to the ground, chastened.

"Don't take it hard, kid, you're still my favorite," Josiah said with a sly grin. "Just speak up, time's wasting."

Jun nodded, then turned around and pointed at a spot on Ndidi's hastily-sketched diagram that had caught her eye.

"What does this represent?" Jun asked, indicating what looked like a set of brackets along the northern side of the bird's-eye-view layout. "Is that a door?"

"In a sense," Ndidi answered, and slid the chart a bit to one side until the side-on-view elevation sketch that she had done earlier was directly in front of her. "It looks to be a rolling door just beside the landing pad I mentioned. Like a big garage door, or the entrance to a hangar?"

Monty leaned over on the other side of the table, still working on a mouthful of food.

"Yeah, I spotted that, too," he said, still chewing. "My first guess was hangar, as well. My thinking is that they designed it so that they could wheel in anything that landed on that pad inside, to get it in out of the elements, or maybe just out of sight."

"But these defensive emplacements you've marked out," Jun went on, pointing at the four corners of the layout, "they're like pillbox turrets facing out?"

"Yes," Ndidi nodded. "With anti-aircraft units on a swivel, each of them looking like they can cover about 270 degrees, covering the approaches more or less directly north, south, east, and west."

Jun had her hand on her chin, a thoughtful expression on her face. The sergeant came over to stand beside her, studying the sketches on the back of the chart for a moment before giving her a sidelong glance.

"What you got cooking, kid?" he asked.

"It just occurred to me that…" She paused, shaking her head. "No, it probably wouldn't work."

"Come on, just spit it out," Josiah urged. "You ever heard the saying, there's no such thing as a bad idea?"

Jun chewed her lower lip for a moment before answering.

"It's just, I think maybe Curtis was right…" she began.

"Okay, now that *is* a bad idea," the sergeant interrupted after a sharp bark of laughter.

"No, I am being serious, sir," Jun pressed on, with more intensity and conviction, not failing to notice Curtis's mock outrage at the sergeant's quip. "Perhaps that landing pad is our best option for entering the structure, after all. Only without powered flight to announce our arrival."

Jun looked up from the chart, and searched the faces of her four squad mates and the three pilots for a glimmer of recognition, but from their expressions it appeared that she was not getting her point across.

"Look," she continued, pointing to each of the four corners of the structures in turn, "the anti-aircraft emplacements are positioned to cover the approaches, but if I'm reading this right then none of the turrets can be turned to face *within*."

Jun paused and glanced to Ndidi for confirmation.

"That is how it appeared to me, yes," the pilot said with a nod.

"And with the fortress built partially into the side of the mountain, that means that the slope continues upwards above the hangar entrance?" Jun ran her fingertip along the wavy lines that Ndidi had sketched in on the north side of the structure in the bird's-eye view, like the gradations in a contour map showing changes in elevation.

"Yeah," Monty chimed in, wiping crumbs from the corners of his mouth, "that's about the size of it, from what I recall."

"It had been my assumption," Sibyl put in, sounding unsure, "that we would attempt to land on the flank of the mountain where the slope is more gradual but the mountainside itself is wider, giving us a broader margin for error in terms of a drop zone. And that we would then make the short ascent to the fortress from below. Correct me if I'm wrong, Jun, but it sounds like you are suggesting the complete opposite."

"I suppose that I am, yes," Jun replied. "Assuming that the winds are with us"—she paused and glanced in Monty's direction, who once again formed an 'x' with his forearms to indicate crosswinds and winced—"we should designate the fortress's landing pad itself our drop zone, with the higher slope as a fallback if circumstances demand. Those emplacements will be watching either for enemy elements climbing up from below or listening for enemy aircraft approaching from above, so if we come in quiet enough and under cover of dark, we just might get down to earth without them noticing."

"And then we knock on the door like Werner here says," Curtis said with a sneer, gesturing in the direction of the German soldier.

"Dear boy, it *was* your suggestion, after all," Sibyl cautioned. "Even if…"

"No, she is right," Werner interrupted, hand on his chin and with a studious expression on his face. "This facility will be staffed by SS zealots, after all. They were indoctrinated to view their enemies as subhuman and beneath contempt, and in my experience they tend to make the mistake of underestimating their opponents as a consequence. Fraulein Jun's plan is so fraught with the potential for disaster that it is almost laughable—"

"Hey, now!" Jun began to object, but Werner motioned for a moment's grace to continue.

"But that is precisely what makes it the most strategic option we could choose," Werner continued. "They will not have been trained to anticipate such an attack because no prudent commander would ever dream of ordering an attack of this sort to be carried out. And ours is most definitely not a prudent commander."

Now it was Josiah's turn to look offended, while Sibyl hid a smile behind her hand and Curtis stifled a chuckle. It took a moment, but Werner finally noticed the expression on the sergeant's face and shrugged his shoulders slightly before continuing.

"I do not mean to give offense, Herr Sergeant, but merely to state the facts. You could hardly be described as being the product of classical military training. And your tactical choices are often not those that a more traditionally-minded and, yes, prudent commander would make."

"Well, I can't exactly argue with that." The sergeant's expression seemed to soften somewhat. Then a smile slowly tugged up the corners of his mouth. "Because that's exactly what we're going to do."

Josiah turned to Hector, who was making a final study of the notations that Ndidi had made to the charts, and copying coordinates and notes over to his clipboard.

"So when do we leave?" the sergeant asked.

Hector finished writing down a few last notes, then flipped the clipboard closed and tucked it under his arm.

"The Wellington is fueled up and prepped for takeoff," he said, standing up straight with shoulders back as if presenting himself for inspection. "If Monty and Ndidi here are willing to assist the ground crew in getting the kite moved into position, we can be ready to takeoff as soon as your team is suited up and kitted out with arms, ammunition, and parachutes. Factoring in the flight time, that should put us over the target in the dead of night, just as planned."

Josiah rubbed his hands together as he turned to address Jun and the rest of the squad.

"Y'all heard the man, right? I want everyone mission-ready and on the airfield in fifteen. So get to it!"

As the rest of the squad trooped out of the mess tent, Jun took one final look at the sketches Ndidi had done of the Alpine fortress. She tried not to think too hard or long about the idea that they would be trying to land in such a relatively small drop zone on her very first parachute jump, much less that it was her idea in the first place.

CHAPTER 16

TWO HOURS LATER, and Jun was still trying not to think too hard about it, but finding it difficult to keep her mind on much of anything else at all. They had been bundled up in the rear of the Vickers Wellington bomber ever since taking off from the base camp's makeshift airfield, sitting on a metal frame affixed to the deck that originally housed the bomber's payload but which had been adapted into rough seating for their use, each of them ineffectively strapped into place by a collection of web belts and netting to prevent them from bouncing from deck to ceiling and back again whenever the plane hit a bit of turbulence. They had to shout to be heard over the sound of the Wellington's twin engines, which thrummed and roared just beyond the plane's hull to either side of them. Not that there was much left for them to discuss, beyond the most obvious questions, none of which they could yet answer. Like a tongue always searching out the sorest tooth, Jun's thoughts continued to circle back around to those questions again and again: Would they survive the parachute jump and successfully reach the ground? Would they manage to reach the drop zone as planned? If they managed to reach the landing pad in one piece and in sure enough health to continue the mission, could they manage to gain access to the fortress itself? And on, and on, and on. The mission before them seemed full of any number of insurmountable difficulties.

But as she had learned when she had first been forced to fight against the Dead on the Eastern Front, Jun knew that the only way to approach a seemingly problem is not to look towards the mission's ultimate goal, but instead to focus only on the next step immediately before you. It did Jun no good to wonder now about possible difficulties they might have gaining access to the fortress's hangar doors, or even to worry about remembering to bend her legs and roll properly when she came in for a landing. Her most pressing concern was with getting out of the plane in one piece and them getting her chute open in time for a controlled descent. Anything beyond that was a problem for a future Jun to concern herself with, once the concerns of the present Jun were a thing of the past.

And so Jun kept her eyes on the bay doors that they would shortly be exiting the plane through, and her hand trailed repeatedly to the ripcord that hung from one side of the harness she wore, that would release the tightly-packed parachute she wore on her back. She tried not to focus on what Hector had said, about paratroopers more traditionally using what he called a "static line," which caused their chutes, or "canopies" as he called them, to open automatically when they jumped from the plane. But he had gone on to explain that the Wellington had not been designed to carry paratroopers, and there wasn't time to attempt rigging up a functional static line in the bomber's bay. With what Jun had come to recognize as Hector's characteristic good humor and optimism, he had simply smiled and told them that they had nothing to worry about, so long as they kept their wits about them and remembered to pull the ripcord roughly five seconds after exiting the plane. Pull it too soon and they'd risk tangling up with one another, and pull it too late and they would run the risk that the chutes would not fully deploy in time to slow their descent to a safe enough speed before they reached the ground.

All of which Jun was studiously trying not to think about as she concentrated all of her attention on the simplest aspects of the task that lay before her, and not on what might go wrong.

Wait your turn, get out of the plane, count to five, then pull the cord. Wait your turn, get out of the plane, count to five, then pull the cord. Again, and again, and again, the words repeated themselves in her mind on a constant loop, like a mantra.

So deeply engrained had they become, and so focused was her attention, that when Josiah tapped her on the shoulder, Jun turned around and began to say them out loud, picking up right where her internal monologue had left off.

"Count to five, then pull the cord," she said by rote, before realizing what she was doing. She stopped herself short, embarrassed.

"How's that, again?" the sergeant shouted over the roar of the engines, tapping the tip of his index finger against the hinge of his jaw just beneath his earlobe. He was standing over Jun, holding onto webbing affixed to the inner hull of the plane and trying his best to maintain his balance. He had evidently just been to the bomber's cockpit and returned. "Couldn't make it out."

"Never mind," Jun said as she shook her head, then when she saw the look of incomprehension on the sergeant's face repeated even louder, shouting "Never mind!"

Josiah shrugged, and then patted her on the shoulder with his free hand.

"I know, I know," he said, managing to sound sympathetic even while shouting, "this whole mess is playing my nerves like a banjo, too, kid. But we'll get through it, if we stick together and stick to the plan. Now, the pilot tells me that we're coming up on the drop zone, so we need to be ready to roll as soon as the bay doors open up. You with me?"

Jun realized that she was nervously chewing her lower lip, and quickly stopped doing so before nodding her assent, her jaw clenched tightly shut.

"Good girl," the sergeant said, patting her once more on the shoulder and then moving on to pass the instructions on to the rest of the squad in turn, beginning with Sibyl to Jun's immediate left.

Through the corner of her eye, Jun could see that Sibyl's normally placid and calm demeanor was slipping, but unlike Jun the Englishwoman did not seem to be worried or concerned about their impending jump. Instead, Sibyl seemed to be positively excited about the idea. Jun couldn't clearly make out what she and the sergeant were saying to one another, but from her manner and the expression that Josiah was wearing as he responded, Jun wouldn't have been surprised to learn that Sibyl was relating some familiar old quotation that her late husband always used to say, or else was recounting how their present circumstances reminded her of some adventure the two of them had shared in their travels before the war.

Leaving Sibyl beaming a happy smile, the sergeant moved down the line to get Curtis up to speed, and while Jun could hear even less of their conversation than she had of the previous one, from the facial expressions and body language of both men it was clear enough to understand what was being said. Curtis was making some wry remark or a cynical quip, and Josiah was playing the long-suffering superior officer trying to get a subordinate to take matters seriously. Considering how often Josiah was the one to share a joke or a tall tale with a humorous twist ending, it always amused Jun to see how often Curtis managed to force the sergeant into the role of his own personal straight man.

Then Josiah had reached the end of the line and was bending down to talk to Werner. Their exchange was the shortest of them all, with the sergeant saying just a few short words and the German soldier replying with nothing more than a curt nod, the consummate professional. No time or energy wasted with unnecessary pleasantries or banter, no chit chat or commentary. They had their orders, and Werner was ready to carry them out when the time came.

And it appeared that the time had come. As Josiah made his way back along the deck towards the forward end of the bay, a light flashed in a wire cage above the hatch to the cockpit. Jun turned, and saw that Hector was leaning over and looking back through the hatch into the bay, holding up one hand and giving them a thumbs up, a big grin on his face. He shouted something to the sergeant that Jun couldn't hear, but the gist of it was clear enough.

It was time to go.

The bomb bay doors clanked loudly as they began to lever open. Jun could feel the vibration through the deck beneath her feet, as the viciously cold air from outside began to blow through the ever-widening gap as the doors continued to open.

From the end of the line, Josiah pointed at Werner and then held up his index finger and spun it in a tight circle, like he was winding up an imaginary flywheel. The German soldier nodded, and quickly extricated himself from the web belts that had held him fastened to their makeshift seating. Securing the bundle of weapons that hung from a strap at the bottom of his parachute's deployment bag, then holding the bundle in front of him, Werner made his way to the edge of the open bomb bay doors. He nodded once in the squad's direction, and then he was through the doors and out of sight.

Curtis had moved into position while Jun's attention was on Werner, and after a delay of mere seconds the young American had gone through the open doors after him. Jun was watching Sibyl move into position when she felt the sergeant's hand on her shoulder.

"We gotta go, kid," the sergeant shouted in her ear. "This is our stop!"

Jun swallowed hard as she carried her own bundle of weapons clutched close to her chest, and hurried across the deck to the edge of the bay doors, reaching it just as Sibyl disappeared from view. She paused for the briefest of instants to glance back over her shoulder at the sergeant who was moving into position directly behind her. Josiah grinned and gave her a thumbs up. Jun nodded, turned to the open doors, and held her breath as she stepped over the edge and plunged down into the night.

CHAPTER 17

JUN CROUCHED IN the shadows at the edge of the landing pad, ears straining to hear any sounds coming from the defensive emplacement that stood about twenty yards to her right. Whenever she shifted her weight her left ankle screamed out in agony, from where she twisted it badly when she landed higher up the slope of the mountain a short time below. She'd had to limp her way down onto the platform, but at least the ankle had not proven to be broken as she'd originally feared.

Of all the members of the squad, only Sibyl and Werner had managed to touch down directly in the designated drop zone, coming down right in the middle of the landing pad itself. Sergeant Josiah had come down even farther up the slope than Jun had, and for a considerable while it looked like Curtis might have been blown off course entirely. It wasn't until Jun and Josiah got out of their harness and rid themselves of their chutes, and then made their way down to the landing pad where they joined Werner and Sibyl, that the young American poked his head up over the edge of the pad, having climbed up from the spot where he'd come down lower on the mountain's slope. And while the squad had suffered the odd scrape or bruise, it appeared that Jun's twisted ankle was the closest any of them had come to an actual injury, and so aside from her pronounced limp the squad was able to move through the shadows unhindered.

Now they waited to see if their arrival had been detected by the fortress's defenses. The squad communicated only in hand gestures and the nod or shake of a head, wary of making any unnecessary noise. Jun listened hard for any sound of klaxons or of voices raised in alarm, but the turrets remained silent. Lights shone from within, but the squad could not see into the interiors from their vantage behind the turrets in the emplacements' blind spots.

When several minutes had passed without any alarm being raised and without guards emerging to defend against invaders, Sergeant Josiah motioned for the squad to approach the hangar doors one by one. He initially signaled for Jun to take the lead, but in response she indicated her injured ankle, suggesting that her limp would slow her down and that she might better serve bringing up the rear, instead. So the sergeant had tapped Werner to take point, with Sibyl and Curtis following close behind. Finally the sergeant darted across the landing pad to the hangar doors, and then Jun trailed after them.

It was only a short distance across the landing pad to the hangar doors, which were even larger than Ndidi's sketched diagram had suggested. By the time that Jun limped her way across the landing pad and reached the others, Werner and the sergeant were already in the process of attempting to lift up the bottom of the rolling door. The intention was that they would force the door to raise just enough for the squad to slide under, while hopefully not making enough noise in the process to alert anyone within to their presence.

Best case scenario would be that they would get the door open and all five of them would be inside before any roaming patrol happened upon them, leaving them free to infiltrate the fortress undetected. Worst case scenario would be that their attempt to open the door would alert someone inside to their presence, and the squad would find themselves facing the full force of the fortress's defenses.

What was actually happening fell somewhere in the middle, Jun decided, better than the worst case but far from the best, as well.

"It won't budge," Josiah said in a harsh whisper, straining to lift the door. He turned and motioned for Curtis and Sibyl to shoulder their arms and join him and Werner in the attempt. But even with another pair of hands they didn't seem able to budge the door even a fraction.

Jun considered adding her own hands to the equation, but took one step closer to the door and winced when her weight shifted onto her injured ankle. She knew that the added strain of attempting to lift the clearly extremely heavy door would be too much for her already complaining joint to take. And so she stayed back, eyes scanning from one side of the landing pad to the other and back, watchful for any enemy forces.

That's when she spotted the shadow in the wall beside the hangar door, not far from the place where she was now standing.

From a distance, and seen in the dim light from the far side of the landing pad, Jun had thought that the rough walls of reinforced concrete to either side of the rolling door continued unbroken until they met the raw stone of the mountainside itself on either side. But from this closer vantage point she could now clearly see that what she had taken to be seams between two sections of the concrete wall was actually some kind of access panel.

Glancing back to see that the sergeant and the others were still trying their luck with the rolling door, Jun limped over to the access panel. It was painted the same flat grey as the concrete wall around it, but seen close up it was clearly a different texture, smooth where the concrete was rough. It was small and square, flush with the ground and rising only about as high as Jun's knees. And when she bent down and tapped a fingernail against it, she could hear a faint metallic ringing sound. She ran her fingers around the edges of the panel, and found that she was able to prise it away a fraction of an inch from the surrounding concrete with only a little effort, but couldn't seem able to make it open up any wider.

Not wanting to raise her voice and draw any undue attention, Jun straightened up and limped back over to where the sergeant and the others were clustered around the hangar door.

"Damn thing's gotta be locked," the sergeant said in a voice scarcely above a whisper. "No way it's *that* heavy."

"Maybe this wasn't the best plan to begin with?" Curtis chimed in, unhelpfully.

Sibyl shot the young American a sharp glance, but Werner had stepped away a bit and was studying the edges of the rolling door.

Jun tapped the sergeant on the elbow, and then when he turned to her she pointed in the direction of the access panel. Jun could see a light coming on in the sergeant's eyes as he nodded and quickly stepped over to stand in front of the panel. She watched as he knelt down, did the same sort of cursory inspection that she had a moment before, and like Jun before him tried to pull the panel loose from the surrounding concrete. He only managed to get it to open marginally wider than Jun had, and she could see frustration lining his face. But then he pulled his combat knife out of its sheath on his belt, rammed the point in between the outer lip of the access panel and the concrete behind it, and working the blade back and forth for less than a minute at several key spots around the edge managed to force the panel completely away from the wall. The sergeant deftly caught the panel before it fell clattering to the ground, and then propped it up against the wall to one side before bending down and peering into the space beyond the opening.

Jun lowered herself down onto her knees beside the sergeant, careful not to put too much weight on her injured ankle as she did. She bent low, the palms of her hands against the ground, and as the sergeant leaned out of the way she moved into the place he had just occupied, looking through the small square opening.

It was a mass of electrical wiring, neatly bound into bundles that ran along the sides of a narrow conduit that snaked away from the opening and deep into the wall beyond. The area immediately on the other side of the opening was as dark as the tomb, but light could be seen dimly shining somewhere beyond the bend. And despite the fact that bundles of wiring were affixed to both sides of the conduit, there was about eighteen inches of clearance down the middle, at least as far down the conduit as she could see.

"Well," Josiah said in a quiet voice, laying a hand on Jun's shoulder as she straightened up from the opening. "At least you can stay off of that bum ankle of yours for a while longer."

Jun had the sinking feeling that she knew just what he was suggesting.

"None of the rest of us could squeeze through," the sergeant continued, and then reached out and laid his hands against the outsides of both of Jun's shoulders, like he was taking a measurement. Then he turned back to the opening, his hands still held that distance apart, and sized it against the clearance down the center of the conduit. "It'd be a bit snug, but I think you could manage it."

Jun was already unslinging her submachine gun from her back and pulling the strap of her bolt-action rifle off her shoulder. Sibyl and Curtis had walked over to join them, and Jun handed them her weapons to mind as she removed anything that served to increase her profile, including the heavy coat she had worn. In the end, she kept the holstered Webley Mk VI belted around her waist, along with the combat knife in its sheath, but all of the rest of her equipment, ammunition, and arms she had given over to her squad mates for safe keeping. She stood in shirt sleeves, teeth chattering in the frigid alpine air.

Werner moved silently across the landing pad to join them, keeping his eyes on the defensive turrets. "No sign that they have spotted us yet," he said in a barely audible hush, "but if they adhere to standard defensive procedures then a sentry patrol is bound to sweep through the area before too much longer. Whatever we do, we need to do it quickly."

At the last minute, Jun opted to remove her boots as well. She was not sure what the conduit passed through or by as it traveled through the wall, but was mindful of the dangers of making too much noise as she shimmied her way through, searching for a way in. And her stockinged feet and bare hands would doubtless produce less noise than her boots clanging against the metal walls of the conduit as she crawled along it. It meant that she was even more conscious of the cold than she had been before, but if it reduced her chances of being detected, then the discomfort would be worth it.

"Find a way into the hangar, and get the doors open," Sergeant Josiah said, quiet enough that only Jun could hear, his hands once more on her shoulders, but this time gripping them firmly in a supportive gesture rather than sizing her up. "Doesn't have to be wide open, either, just high enough for us to slide under. You get that?"

Jun just nodded, eyes narrowed. She clenched her jaw, but as much to keep her teeth from chattering from the cold as anything. She found that she was actually eager to get moving, if it meant getting in out of the chill.

"Good luck, then, kid." The sergeant released his hold on her shoulders and stepped aside, waving an arm towards the opening like a doorman at a posh hotel welcoming a guest to enter.

Crouching down low on her hands and knees, Jun crawled to the open access panel. The sergeant was right, it *would* be a tight fit. She felt lucky that she had never been bothered by confined spaces. Or by the dark, as once she was inside the conduit with her body blocking the faint illumination from outside, then the only source of the light would be somewhere out of sight beyond the last bend ahead.

Pushing her arms out in front of her, palms down against the cold metal floor of the conduit, she slid forward as far as she was able, until she was sliding along on her stomach. Then using her hands to pull and her feet to push, she shimmied her way through the narrow opening in the conduit, gradually inching her way into the heart of the fortress.

CHAPTER 18

CRAWLING THROUGH THE confined space felt a little too much like being buried alive in a narrow coffin, and Jun had not travelled far along the conduit's length before she regretting thinking only moments earlier that snaking through the cramped, dark space would be preferable to being out in the open, chill air. And while she was not normally one given to unnecessary fears, something about being so constricted, with her mobility so severely limited, was bringing out any number of anxieties and worries that would not usually have even occurred to her.

Her pulse thundered in her ears, and the sound of her own breathing seemed near deafening as it echoed back to her off the cold metal walls of the passageway. She found herself wondering if the air supply within the conduit might be limited, and if so if she might be in danger of exhausting it before she made it through. At one point she even thought to wonder whether any of the bundles of cables she was brushing past might be improperly insulated, and from that moment onwards part of her brain was occupied with worries about being electrocuted by coming into contact with a bare live wire.

After what had only been a matter of minutes but felt like a small eternity, Jun finally reached the bend in the conduit that she had seen from outside, beyond which a light was shining somewhere ahead. Thankfully the bend in the conduit was a fairly gradual one, Jun realized with a sigh of relief, as she would likely have had considerable difficulty pushing herself through had it been a turn that was any sharper. As it was, there was a moment after her head and shoulders were past the turn but her lower half was still on the far side, where she had to hold her breath and suck in her gut as much as possible to squeeze her hips through the turn. But then she was all of the way past, and could at last see what the source of the illumination ahead was.

The conduit continued straight beyond the bend for at least another twenty or thirty feet before turning again, but about halfway along that length there was some kind of metal grill set into the right side of the conduit. Bright light streamed in through the gaps in the metal grill, shafts of illumination carving up the darkness within the narrow space.

It took Jun several more minutes to drag and push herself along the conduit until she approached the grill, and every minute that it took, every second that passed, she was conscious of the rest of the squad standing out in the open on the landing pad, exposed not only to the elements but to the view of any patrol that might happen randomly to pass by. Her muscles screamed in agony over the odd contortions she was forcing them into, the skin of her palms rubbed raw by the friction. Her injured ankle was already a constant source of pain and distress, but now her toes on both feet felt battered and abused, and she wouldn't be surprised to learn that she had managed to dislocate one or more of them in the process.

But finally her head and shoulders pulled even with the edge of the metal grill, and squinting her eyes Jun was able to peer through the tiny gaps in the grill and into the brightly-lit space beyond.

At first, all she could see was the broad expanse of concrete that stretched out just below the other side of the grill, the floor of the hangar inside the rolling door. Then, shifting her weight up onto one shoulder and craning her neck to one side, she could see the rolling hangar door itself, and twisting around as far as she was able she could just make out the chain-and-pulley system on the sides of the hangar door which winched it up and open. Lowering herself back onto both shoulders, her cheek pressed against the metal floor of the conduit, Jun tried to see if there was anyone about in the hangar, but as far as she could see, the cavernous space was entirely empty.

Gritting her teeth, Jun got to work on trying to remove the grill from the opening, remaining careful not to make any unnecessary noise. Just because she couldn't see anyone in the hangar didn't mean that there wasn't anyone there. The view from her vantage point seemed almost as restricted as her range of motion within the conduit itself, which was making removing the grill even more difficult than she had anticipated. She found the places where screws had been driven into place from the other side, affixing the grill to a metal frame that sat in the side wall of the conduit. In the end, she found that it was more manageable simply to remove the entire frame, grill and all, using the point of her combat knife to bend back the somewhat more malleable metal of the conduit wall, gradually freeing the grill and frame from their moorings.

The frame and grill came loose a split second

sooner than Jun had anticipated, while she still had both hands on the handle of her combat knife, bending back the last bit of the conduit wall holding it in place. The heavy grill landed on the concrete floor beyond with a deafening clatter, that echoed back from the far walls of the hangar, reverberating in the enormous space.

Jun cringed, shoulders hunched, sure that at any moment guards would come rushing over to investigate. But as the last faint echoes of the clattering grill died away, the hangar once more settled into a still silence.

Deciding that either the coast was clear or it would soon be too late to do anything about it one way or another, Jun went to work trying to twist and contort herself to squeeze through the open gap in the wall of the conduit. It was even a tighter fit than climbing into the conduit had been in the first place, made even more difficult by the fact that there were now bits of twisted metal with sharp edges where Jun had pried the grill's frame loose from its housing. As it was, Jun managed to wiggle her way almost entirely through the gap before suffering an injury, when one of the sharp bits of twisted metal dug into the outside of her right thigh as she squeezed through.

Jun was through the gap and on her hands and

knees, her eyes having to adjust to the bright illumination in the hangar after the dim gloom within the conduit. Her Webley revolver was in her hand even before she had climbed to her feet, her eyes darting to either side of her, ears straining to hear the sound of approaching footsteps. And while she could hear a voice echoing somewhere in the distance, too far to make out any individual words but with a buzzing electronic quality to it that suggested it was someone talking over a loud-speaker or through a public address system, the hangar itself remained quiet.

She took a brief moment to check on her thigh. The metal had torn through the fabric of her fatigue pants, but while it did drag a nasty gash across her thigh deep enough to draw blood, the wound was shallow enough that Jun didn't think that it needed immediate dressing.

Now that she had a less restricted view, Jun was able to get a better sense of the layout of the hangar. The rolling doors were to her right, with the chain-and-pulley assembly that she had seen along one side. The floor of the hangar was concrete, and on the far side of the hangar were stacked metal drums of what looked to be gasoline, and a rack of automotive tools in the adjacent corner. Far to her left Jun could see a set of reinforced metal doors that appeared to lead to a corridor beyond, and it was through these that the amplified voice appeared to be issuing.

To her immediate left was a small control room, with leaded windows reinforced with metal wires that looked out over the hangar floor. The door to this control room stood open, and inside Jun could see a bank of dials and switches and levers. Keeping her Webley at the ready and crouching low, Jun hurried to the open door to the control room. After making certain that it was empty, she slipped inside, and studied the controls. And while her German vocabulary was minimal, she was able to make out the words for "door" and "open" above one of the larger levers.

Holding her breath, Jun took hold of the lever and eased it up. With an electronic hum and a clanking sound far overhead, the chain-and-pulley began to grind into motion, and the hangar doors slowly inched open.

Sure that the sound would bring guards rushing at any moment, Jun held the lever in position for only a matter of seconds, just long enough for the bottom edge of the hangar door to lift about three feet up off of the concrete floor. Then she let go and the lever immediately slammed back into the off position.

Then she slipped back out of the control room and crouched low in the corner, her Webley trained on the reinforced metal doors in the wall to her left. If guards came rushing in to investigate the sound of the opening door while Jun's squad mates were still slipping inside, she would at least be in a position to cover them long enough for them to take up defensive positions and defend themselves.

But by the time the sergeant and the others were through the three-foot gap beneath the bottom of the rolling door and at Jun's side, the reinforced metal doors had remained closed, and the only sound she could hear was that of the amplified voice from the other side.

"Good work, kid," the sergeant said in a quiet voice as he handed Jun's boots back to her. Jun holstered her revolver and then sat down, pulling on one boot and then the other, wincing as she tightened the laces over her injured ankle, trying to ignore the icy traceries of pain from the cut on her thigh. "Run into any trouble?"

Jun shook her head as she climbed to her feet, and then accepted her coat and then her weapons and ammunition from Sibyl and Curtis, while the sergeant and Werner kept their guns trained on the metal doors to one side and the partially-open hangar door on the other.

"Should we close that thing behind us?" Curtis said, jerking a thumb over his shoulder at the rolling door.

"Looks like we got lucky and no one heard us coming in, but I don't want to make any more noise we don't have to," the sergeant said, shaking his head. "And besides, could be that we'll want to make a hasty exit, and it'd be nice not to have to slow down and open it up again, if we did decide to close it."

"There is the chance that a patrol outside might notice the light spilling out," Werner said cautiously, "or that someone in one of the turrets might see it."

"That's a risk we'll have to take," the sergeant replied. "'Cause boxing ourselves in here without an easy way back out is an even bigger risk."

Jun had finished strapping back on all of her equipment, and took a moment to tie a bandana around the cut on her thigh. It would serve well enough until she had time to dress the wound properly. She only hoped that it didn't get infected before she had a chance to see to it. Then she hoped that she lived long enough even to need to worry about an infection in the first place. But they had more pressing concerns.

"Everyone ready to move out," the sergeant

asked, speaking to all of the squad but clearly mostly interested in Jun's response.

Jun just nodded in reply, lips pressed tightly shut. She felt a little more secure with the weight of her submachine gun in her hands, to say nothing of the sense of strength in numbers that being back with the squad gave her.

"Then what are we waiting for, y'all?" The sergeant treated her to a lopsided grin before motioning for the squad to advance. They were headed towards the reinforced metal doors, and whatever lay beyond. "Let's see what we can see, shall we?"

CHAPTER 19

STEALTH WAS OF the essence at this stage of the operation. Their primary objectives were threefold: to infiltrate the Alpine Fortress; determine whether there was anyone at the site capable of directing the attacks of the Dead forces against the Resistance; and if so, to locate and eliminate that command structure. They had so far managed to accomplish the first objective without meeting active resistance, but as they made their way deeper into the fortress Jun had every expectation that they would encounter enemy elements at any turn. But after checking through the branching corridors on the top level of the structure and then continuing down the stairs to the next highest, they did not meet anyone at all. The upper levels of the fortress appeared to be deserted, though the lights shone in every room and down the full length of every corridor.

They could *hear* someone, though. The amplified voice that Jun had heard coming from the other side of the reinforced doors when she first entered the hangar had continued to deliver a lengthy address unabated since they had entered the structure, broadcast through the fortress via a public address system, with speakers mounted high on the walls every dozen paces or so along the corridor. With her limited German she was only able to pick up the occasional word or phrase, but it was clearly an impassioned speech about the noble future of the Reich, with references to the "flower of German youth" and "purity" and "vitality."

They were close to finishing their check of the second floor down from the top, and the speech continued to blare from the buzzing speakers overhead.

"Does that joker *ever* shut up?" Curtis sneered, jabbing the barrel of his M1 Carbine at the nearest of the loudspeakers.

"He would have shut up for good," Werner said in a low voice, a stern expression on his face, "if I'd taken the shot when I still had the chance."

Jun and the others stopped and looked back in the German soldier's direction. He saw their perplexed expression and replied with a curt shrug.

"*This* is the bloody-handed bastard," Werner

explained, stretching out his arm and pointing a finger angrily at the speaker, scowling deeply. "The man speaking now is the one I should have killed when I had the chance: Standartenführer Hermann Ziegler."

"Nice of you to share that little tidbit," the sergeant drawled. "Better late than never, I suppose."

Werner lowered his hand and tightened his grip on the handle of his MP40, and it seemed to Jun that his expression was uncharacteristically sheepish.

"Yes, you are right, Herr Sergeant," he answered, lowering his eyes to the ground. "I should have indicated that our intel that Ziegler was in command of this installation was correct as soon as I recognized his voice when we entered the facility. But I…"

Werner's hands had tightened into a white-knuckled grip on his weapon, as though it was a wet cloth that he was attempting to wring the moisture from, eyes flashing darkly as his sheepish expression was replaced by a mask of tightly controlled rage. Jun found it a little unsettling, seeing the typically calm and possessed Werner, always the model of the professional, displaying such naked emotion.

"At ease, soldier," Josiah said. "I get it. You have history with the man, and I can respect that. Let's just stay focused on the mission at hand."

Relaxing his grip on the MP40 fractionally, Werner nodded, but the angry expression that lined his face did not seem to soften much at all. Whatever unpleasant memories were currently circling behind those flashing eyes, whatever atrocities Werner had witnessed that had been brought back to mind by the sound of the Waffen-SS colonel's voice over the loudspeaker... Jun could scarcely imagine what horrors they must have been, considering the things that she had seen the German soldier take in stride in their time serving together. And she recognized the unfamiliar glimmers that she saw now flashing across Werner's face as an appetite for vengeance.

At the end of the corridor they found another set of stairs leading down to the next floor below. They eased their way down the steps, careful not to make any unnecessary noise, but when they reached the door at the bottom of the stairs they found it locked. There was nothing to be gained by backtracking the way that they'd come, since the only other stairs that they'd passed were the short series of steps leading back up to the top level that they'd originally entered through the doors in the hangar. The locked door was their only means of accessing the rest of the fortress.

Sergeant Josiah had his hand on his chin, looking thoughtful as he mulled over the possibilities of either shooting through the lock or blowing the door off of its hinges, neither of which seemed particularly likely outcomes to Jun. At best, such an approach would mean that they would alert everyone on the floor beyond of their arrival if they did manage to force the door down in the first place.

"Here, Josiah dear, let me take a crack at it," Sibyl said, tapping the sergeant on the shoulder and slipping past him. She bent down to get a better look at the lock in the door, than unbuttoned the flap on the breast pocket of her jacket, and pulled out a small canvas bundle about the size of her outstretched palm. She unrolled the bundle, and pulled out a pair of small metal picks.

As Sibyl bent down and inserting the first of the picks into the keyhole on the door's lock, Curtis shook his head, whistling low.

"Why, Mrs. Beaton, I'm *shocked*," the young American said. "A respectable lady like yourself, a garden-variety picklock?"

"Pshaw, dear boy," Sibyl said, holding the first pick in place with one hand and then using the other to maneuver the second pick, turning it in some increments as she sought out each of the tumblers in turn. "Nothing garden-variety about my lock-picking abilities. Our Chester learned the trick of it when he was still at Oxford, and needed to break into the locked desk of a teaching assistant to pull off a prank. But Chester always said I took to it much quicker than he ever did. Said it was all down to…"

There was a final "click" as the last tumbler was twitched into position, and Sibyl smiled as she took hold of the door handle and quietly eased it open.

"All it takes is a woman's touch," she said, smiling sweetly.

"Good work," the sergeant said with a nod in her direction, and then stepped past her to move through the now open door. "Look alive, people. We're bound to run into hostiles sooner rather than later."

As Jun and the others followed the sergeant through the door and into the corridor beyond, she immediately sensed a difference from the two floors above. The top two floors of the structure had seemed deserted, had still seemed somehow relatively orderly, as if the people who normally lived or worked in those rooms had simply stepped out for a moment and could return at any time.

This new floor, however, was something else entirely.

There was a sense of wrongness here. The air on this floor had a musty smell to it, and dust motes danced thick as soup through the shafts of light shining down from the lights overhead. And the quality of the light itself was different, seeming to have an unhealthy, sickly quality to it, with a queasy yellowish-green tint. The voice of the Waffen-SS colonel still buzzed from the speakers overhead, but his words here sounded muffled and strained, as if they were being heard underwater or from some great distance.

"What's that?" Sibyl said, crouching low as she pointed towards the ceiling a short distance down the corridor.

Jun spun around, raising the barrel of her submachine gun. But Werner, who had already aimed his Karabiner and taken aim, was relaxing visibly, lowering his rifle's barrel.

"It is not a weapon," he said, indicating the metal cylinder mounted on a swivel where the wall met the ceiling. "It is a camera. Closed circuit, with the imagery feeding to a central control center somewhere in the facility, for security and surveillance. The German army began using them to monitor rocket test launches in Peenemunde during the war. I noticed a few of them placed high on the interior walls of the hangar as we entered, no doubt used to keep watch over the comings and goings of aircraft in the facility remotely."

Jun couldn't tell if Werner intended the tone of superiority that crept into his voice as he explained what the camera was, or if she was hearing something that wasn't there. As much as he despised what the so-called Führer and the SS cult that followed him had done to Werner's beloved Fatherland, there were still occasions where one could clearly see the deep-seated pride that Werner still felt for his native country. Perhaps the tension between that deep-seated pride and the shame he felt was the engine that fueled that rage and hunger for vengeance that Jun had seen in his face.

"Does that mean that someone's watching us right now?" Curtis asked uncertainly, looking up at the camera with an uneasy expression.

Werner shrugged. "It is certainly a strong possibility. I would suggest that we err on the side of caution and proceed with the assumption that our presence has been noted, yes."

The sergeant motioned for the squad to continue, and they carried on down the corridor. The next set of doors they came to were closed, but on inspection turned out not to be locked. Inside they found a large room filled with metal bunks bolted to the concrete floor, but that was otherwise empty.

Sibyl had hung back, and was standing beneath the surveillance camera mounted high on the wall, looking up and examining it closely. When the sergeant glanced back and saw that she had stayed behind, he gestured to get her attention.

"You spot something?" he asked.

Sibyl pointed at the camera overhead, and then at a bunch of cables that ran from its swivel mount and along the top edge of the wall, continuing down the length of the corridor and then disappearing around a turn.

"If these cameras do feed to a central control center as suggested," the Englishwoman observed, taking pains not to mention Werner or even look in his direction, "then surely that's where these cables lead to, no?"

Curtis had moved further down the corridor, and stopped beneath another surveillance camera mounted on the wall near a junction with another hallway that branched off to one side. "Looks like the cables from this one are headed in the same direction, sarge."

"Good catch, y'all," the sergeant answered, nodding first in Sibyl's direction and then towards Curtis. "And it stands to reason that whoever is calling the shots here is either at that command center or can be reached from it. So let's follow that trail of bread crumbs and see where it leads."

They continued down the corridor, following the path of the cables from the surveillance cameras.

"Sarge," Curtis said, sounding uneasy, "isn't the idea to leave a trail of bread crumbs so you can find your way back *out* of the deep, dark, scary forest?"

"Listen, kid," Josiah answered with a sly smile, "you mix your metaphors how you like, and let me mix mine my own self."

"Okay," the young American said with a dramatic sigh, "but don't come crying to me if we get caught in some damned gingerbread house or some such nonsense."

Jun didn't understand half of what either of them was saying, but didn't much notice. She was too busy studying their surroundings as they advanced deeper into the structure. The sense of wrongness that had assailed her since they had first reached this floor was only intensifying the farther in they travelled, and the warbling voice of the Waffen-SS colonel droning on from the loudspeakers only served to increase that unease.

Werner had taken point as they moved through the next juncture where hallways and corridors branched away from one another, and was following the path of the cameras' cables as they snaked from one corridor through the next. He pulled up short, motioning the squad to come to an immediate halt with a fist held over his shoulder.

"I believe that we have found it," he said simply, and with the barrel of his rifle gestured down one of the wider corridors leading away from the intersection.

Jun looked, and could see wires snaking along the tops of multiple halls and corridors, all converging in a junction box directly above a heavy reinforced metal door.

"Let's open her up and take a look." Sergeant Josiah motioned for the squad to spread out as they approached. Curtis and Werner took up positions on one side of the door, with the sergeant pressed against the wall on the other side. The sergeant reached over, took hold of the door handle, and gingerly tried to turn it, but while the handle turned freely the door refused to budge. "Locked," he said in a whisper, and nodded towards Sibyl. "Do your thing."

Sibyl knelt down to examine the lock, while Jun hung back to guard their rear.

"It's a different sort of lock but I think I can manage it," the Englishwoman said in a quiet voice, and went to reach for the canvas bundle in her pocket. But before she could pull it out they were interrupted by the sound of approaching footsteps, echoing from down one of the branching hallways.

"What do you see, kid?" the sergeant called over to Jun, who was still guarding the rear.

No, not echoes, Jun realized. There were steps approaching from *several* of the hallways that met at the intersection of corridors. And all of them growing louder by the second, threatening to drown out the sound of the warbling voice buzzing from the loudspeakers overhead.

"Trouble," Jun answered simply, just as the first of the Dead came shambling around the corner, bony hands out and grasping, jaws working feverishly as it hungered for the flesh of the living.

CHAPTER 20

"SERGEANT?" JUN CALLED back over her shoulder without taking her eyes off the zombie staggering around the corner. If they were still operating in stealth mode, trying to avoid calling attention to themselves, then opening fire with a Thompson M1A1 in an enclosed space was bound to put an end to that plan.

It took the sergeant a split second to understand that she was waiting for permission to open fire, as he paused a moment before hastily shouting back, "Shoot it already, dammit!"

Jun placed a round from her submachine gun squarely in the head of the shambler, dropping it in its tracks. But before it had even hit the floor more of the Dead came rounding the corner behind it, with still more emerging from several of the other corridors that met at the intersection.

"Put the bastards down!" Sergeant Josiah called

out, stepping away from the still-locked door and raising his 12-gauge shotgun, firing a round at the nearest of the Dead and working the pump to chamber another round. "They know we're here now, so make as much noise as you like!"

Within the span of heartbeats, the hallways echoed with the sound of the squad's gunfire and the inhuman shrieks of the oncoming Dead. There were already nearly a half-dozen fallen corpses of the undead rotting on the ground at their feet by the time that Sibyl unslung her Lee Enfield Mk III from her shoulder and took aim at one of the zombies staggering into view around the corner. Curtis and Werner had both bagged one each, and Jun was already taking aim on her third target.

One of the faster moving zombies emerged from the pack, charging forward towards Jun, shrieking as it reached out grasping hands towards her. Jun, who had just fired off a round at one of the slower moving shamblers, stumbled back as the quick-moving Dead raced towards her, and she struggled to draw a bead on its head. She squeezed off a short burst from her Thompson that caught the Dead high on its right side, carrying away a big chuck of rotting flesh and bone splinters from its shoulder but doing little to slow its forward momentum. A fleeting bout of panic flashed through Jun's mind, but she bore down and refused to give into it. As the Dead closed the gap between them, Jun changed tactics, quickly side-stepping as the Dead lunged towards her and then rearing back and bashing it in the side of its head with the stock of her submachine-gun. The force of the impact knocked the zombie off balance, and its bony arms pinwheeled as it struggled to keep its feet on the ground while trying to regain its equilibrium. Not that Jun was about to give it the opportunity. With a deft motion she spun the Thompson back around, shoved its barrel almost point blank against the back of the zombie's skull, and squeezed the trigger.

Rotted grey matter, black blood, and ropey viscera sprayed on the floor of the corridor as the front of the Dead's face exploded in a shower of bone fragments and gore, and the nearly-decapitated body dropped motionless to the floor at Jun's feet.

But Jun didn't even pause for a moment to be relieved that she'd so narrowly avoided being slashed by one of the zombies, not when still more were following close in its wake. Instead she spun around and fired off another short burst from the Thompson at the next of the Dead in range. When it dropped motionless to the floor as well, there was a moment's pause as the squad stood poised and ready to fire on the next zombie to come into view.

And then they waited another moment, that seemed to stretch out without end.

"I think maybe that's—" Curtis began, but Jun cut him off with a quick motioned.

"Footsteps approaching," Jun said simply, sweeping the barrel of her Thompson back and forth from one branch of the intersection to another to another as she tried to work out from which direction the echoing footsteps she could hear were coming.

Suddenly, a lone zombie shambled into view from the middle corridor before them, mouth working soundlessly, bony hands out and grasping.

The zombie all but exploded in the hail of gunfire as all five members of the squad opened fire on it in the same instant. Shotgun blast, submachine gun fire, and rifle rounds tore into it, shredding the Dead where it stood.

The echoes of the barrage were still reverberating through the corridor as the destroyed remains of the last zombie collapsed in a heap on the floor along with the decaying remains of the Dead who had fallen before it.

After a long pause, Curtis spoke open, continuing

where he had left off earlier. "So maybe *that* was the last of them?"

Jun strained her ears to listen for the sound of other footsteps approaching. She could just make out the faint noise of movement somewhere far off. It was definitely on the same level that the squad currently occupied, and sounded as if it might be getting louder, but was still faint enough that it was clear that there would be some time before whomever it was—whether living sentry or security patrol, or more undead lackeys—arrived at their current position. And when she said as much to the sergeant, he quickly agreed with her.

"There's not much left to be gained in subtlety, I don't expect. Whoever is running the show knows we're here now, so we don't have any time to lose," Josiah said, eyes narrowed and jaw set. He nodded in Sibyl's direction and pointed at the locked door beneath the junction box where the surveillance camera feeds converged. "Let's get this damned door down and have ourselves a little chat with whoever we find on the other side, what do you say?"

Sibyl just nodded in return, slung her rifle once more over her shoulder, and pulled the canvas bundle with her picks out of her pocket one last time. The squad once again took up position around the door, though this time the sergeant and Curtis stood close by Sibyl's flank with their weapons aimed at the door, ready to contend with anyone who might rush out when the door finally opened, while Jun and Werner took up defensive positions a few paces out, training their eyes and attention on the branching corridors, ready for the sudden arrival of any more of the Dead or of their living masters.

The voice that had droned on and on over the loudspeakers since they entered the facility appeared to have fallen silent, and Jun wondered whether Standartenführer Ziegler's lengthy speech had been interrupted by news of the squad's presence in the fortress. She couldn't say for certain, since the sound of the shrieking zombies and the deafening echoes of the squad's barrage of gunfire would have drowned out the muffled sounds of his voice during the recent encounter, but she was fairly certain that she could still hear his voice shortly before the first of the Dead rounded the corner and attacked them, and by the time the squad stood straining to hear the sound of any more approaching footsteps after the last the oncoming zombies had fallen, the voice over the public address system had fallen silent. Was he on the other side of the reinforced door that Sibyl was even know trying to break into, listening to their attempts to gain entry from the other side?

But just as it appeared that Sibyl was about to finish the work of opening the door, the sound of the Waffen-SS colonel could again be heard buzzing over the loudspeakers up and down the corridors, addressing the faithful Nazi troopers in the fortress, wherever they might be. Again Jun could pick out the odd German word or phrase here and there, about "pride" and "purity" and the "flower of German youth" and so on.

Werner muttered something that Jun couldn't quite make out under his breath, and when she turned to look over in his direction she could see a puzzled expression on his face. She was about to ask him to translate when the expression on his face was immediately replaced by one of wary concentration, as he turned and raised the barrel of his MP40 and aimed it at one of the hallways branching away from the intersection a short distance away from their position.

"Someone is coming," the German soldier said simply, finger resting on the trigger guard, eyes trained on the gloom beyond the bend.

Jun turned her attention that way as well, and after listening for a moment she could hear the sound of someone approaching as well. They were still a ways off, but getting closer by the second.

"Any time now would be good, lady," Sergeant Josiah said to Sibyl, an urgent undertone to his words.

"I'm working, I'm working!" Sibyl answered as best she could with one of her lock picks clamped between her front teeth. She was evidently having a little difficulty finding just the right length and bend of pick to maneuver the tumblers in the lock into place.

The sounds of approaching movement down from the far hallway were growing louder by the moment, as the voice of Standartenführer Ziegler droned on and on over the buzzing loudspeakers. The air around Jun felt stifling and close, with the musty scent of decay heavy in her nostrils. She found herself longing for the cold clarity of the fresh air they'd left behind when entering the fortress, despite the biting chill of the night winds. Would she live long enough to find the sting of the alpine wind against her cheek again, or would her journey end here, deep within this mountainside in this place of hidden menace?

Jun was shaken from her reverie by the sound of the final tumbler clicking into place and the lock in the reinforced door popping open.

"Got it!" Sibyl said in triumph as she plucked

the lock pick from between her teeth and shoved it back in the canvas bundle with the others. She quickly climbed to her feet and stepped aside as Sergeant Josiah moved into position directly in front of the door, reaching out and taking hold of the handle.

The sounds of approaching footsteps were growing louder, and Jun was sure that the next wave of attackers would be on them at any moment.

"Eyes up," Josiah said, and reached down to take hold of the door's handle with his left hand, his Colt M1911 semiautomatic pistol gripped tightly in his right. The hinges were on their side, meaning that the door would need to be pulled open rather than bursting through, and either way they would be exposing themselves to gunfire from anyone standing ready on the other side the second the door was opened. The sergeant had clearly taken all of this into account, especially considering the fact that he would be putting himself in the line of fire before asking anyone else in the squad to do so. "Keep low, move fast, try to take them alive."

The door slammed open as the sergeant yanked on the handle, and Werner immediately dove through, his MP40 held in a two-handed grip before him and ready to fire. Josiah was next through the door, crouching low and diving to the left, while Curtis and Sibyl moved quickly to the right. Jun was the last through, still keeping one eye on the intersection of corridors behind them and half of her attention on the footsteps that were growing ever closer.

The room beyond the door was dimly lit, illuminated almost exclusively by the faint blue glow of a bank of screens mounted on the right hand wall. It was a fairly small room, the air still and calm with the faint ozone scent of electrical systems humming away. With the door open, Jun could now clearly hear the voice of Standartenführer Ziegler reciting his speech in German, and as she moved into the room she saw that he was sitting in a swivel chair on the far side of the room with his back to the door, speaking into a large microphone connected to a bank of electrical controls in front of him. And despite the fact that the squad had just burst into his formerly secured space, the Waffen-SS colonel did not seem to take any notice of their arrival, continuing his speech without pause.

The sound of another wave of approaching Dead could now be clearly heard approaching from just the other side of the door.

"Sir?" Jun called over, as the sergeant and Werner slowly approached Standartenführer Ziegler from behind, their weapons held at the ready. "We've got incoming hostiles."

"Then get that door shut and locked," Josiah called back without taking his eyes off the SS colonel, who had yet to as much as turn back and look in their direction. The sergeant pointed the barrel of his Colt at the back of Ziegler's head, at almost pointblank range. "Enough with the speechifying, you Nazi bastard, we've got some questions for you."

Werner stepped in and put a hand on the sergeant's shoulder. "Do not bother, Herr Sergeant."

Josiah glanced over at him with a confused expression. In response, Werner lowered his weapon, then reached out and took hold of the back of Ziegler's chair, and with a short shove spun it around so that the colonel was facing them.

The speech continued unabated, while the corpse of Standartenführer Ziegler sat silently, mouth hanging open, sightless eyes looking out over eternity in a sunken-cheeked face. It was clear that the colonel had been dead for a long, long time.

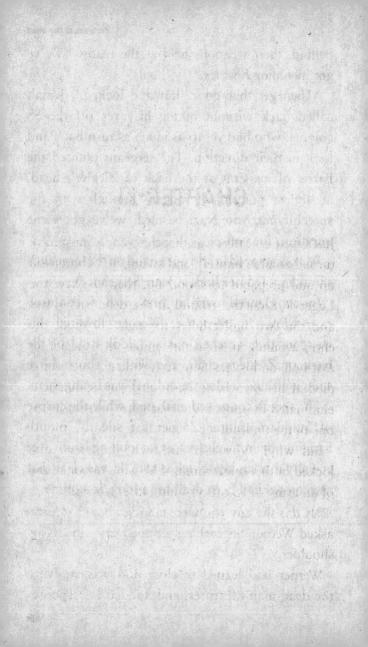

CHAPTER 21

JUN'S FIRST REACTION was that the colonel must have turned zombie himself, and swung her Thompson up and prepared to shoot. But then she saw the Luger P08 on the ground at the dead man's feet and the two bullet holes through his skull, the entry wound on his right temple and the larger exit hole on his left. Standartenführer Ziegler had died at his own hand, and with a headshot that eliminated the possibility that he would return as one of the undead.

But why? Why take his own life, alone and locked in this small room, if he were in command of an army of SS officers and Hitler Youth?

"Is *this* the guy you were talking about?" Curtis asked Werner, his carbine propped casually on his shoulder.

Werner had leaned in close and was studying the dead man's features, and nodded in response.

"Yes, this is Ziegler."

"But I thought you said that you recognized him talking over the P.A.," Curtis persisted, a confused expression on his face as he gestured toward the ceiling, and the speakers from which the voice was still droning on, "and you'll excuse me saying, but I don't figure this joker has been in a talking mood for a *long* while."

"I may have an answer to that." Sibyl had stepped closer to the wall of switches and controls not far from the swivel chair where the dead man's body was sitting. She indicated two platters of a reel-to-reel wire recorder that were rotating at a glacial pace, and then reached over and flipped the switch beside them. And as the platters gradually slowed to a halt, the voice over the loudspeakers grew slower and deeper until it fell silent altogether as the platters finally stopped moving entirely. "The old boy was speaking from beyond the grave, as it were."

"I suspected it was a recording when he began reciting the same speech from the beginning, word for word," Werner said, which explained the odd expression that Jun had seen on his face after the voice had begun speaking again after a short pause.

Sergeant Josiah walked over to take a closer look at the body of Standartenführer Ziegler, while

Werner's attentions turned to a sheaf of papers on the desk in front of the swivel chair where they had found the body sitting.

"So he locks himself in here," Josiah said, "records a stirring speech about the future of the Third Reich, and then tops himself with a bullet through the brain pan. Does that about size things up? What kind of plan is that?"

Werner picked up the top sheets from the stack, and from where Jun was standing she could see that they were covered in neat rows of handwritten notes. A log of some kind, perhaps?

"Ah," Werner said as he read from the pages, his eyebrows raising fractionally as he did. He finished the top page, then flipped to the next, his gaze quickly scanning row after row of text. His expression darkened the longer he read, eyes narrowing as his brow furrowed in anger. Then he swore under his breath in German, scowling.

"Something you'd care to share with the rest of the class, Werner?" Josiah asked, glancing over in his direction. "Shed any light on our little predicament here, does it?"

"Some, perhaps," Werner answered through gritted teeth. "This is the final log of Standartenführer Ziegler, who was indeed in command of an entire division sent up here to wait out the fall of Berlin and then continue to wage war against the Reich's enemies as long as circumstances required. The rumors of the Alpine Redoubt were true, it appears, as was the account we were given by the villagers... up to a point, at least."

"What point would that be?" the sergeant asked, arching an eyebrow in a quizzical expression.

"Ziegler had enough men and arms to carry out large scale assaults on multiple targets for *years*, and enough food and supplies to house all of them here indefinitely. But that all changed after Plan Z was enacted."

"So he *was* able to control the Dead, after all?" Jun asked, breathless.

Werner shook his head before answering.

"Quite the contrary, actually," he explained. "Ziegler's account is confused, and the details are difficult to pick apart, but it is clear that some number of the Dead got into the fortress in those early days after Plan Z, and tore their way through the men stationed here. In short order, the facility was overrun with the Dead. Though he was a high-ranking officer in the S.S., Ziegler was not in the inner circle of the occult conspiracy, and was ignorant about just how difficult the Dead would be to control. With the aid of his top officers was able to force a number of the Dead out of the facility and out onto the mountainside, and sealed the hangar doors shut behind them…"

"Could be those were the Dead who came down the mountain and attacked our villager friends?" Josiah put in. "Assuming it took them wandering around for a few months to find the place?"

"It would track," Werner answered. "But Ziegler had underestimated the number of Dead that still remained to be dealt with inside the facility. He and his officers successfully managed to clear the top two levels of the fortress, but when they reached this floor they were overwhelmed by the superior numbers of the SS troops and Hitler Youth who had joined the ranks of the Dead. In the end, Ziegler was the only one who managed to reach this control center in one piece, and he barricaded himself within. It seems that his initial plan was to remain here in safety while his surviving troops contended with the infestation of the Dead, and he recorded a stirring speech exhorting them to victory to cheer them along. But it quickly became apparent that all hope was lost."

Werner bent down and picked up the Luger P08, and with a sour expression tossed it onto the desk with the dead man's handwritten log.

"And in the end, Ziegler took the coward's way out. All of the atrocities he oversaw in his lifetime, all of the evil he was directly and indirectly responsible for bringing into the world, and this is where it all led. A sad and frightened little man cowering here in the dark, listening to his own flowery speech about the noble future of his hateful regime, while the flower of German youth and vitality is left to rot in the darkness on the other side of the door..."

He then moved to stand over the dead man's corpse, glaring down at its wizened features.

"I should have killed you myself when I had the chance," Werner snarled. He spat in the dead man's face, and then turned and walked away.

"So the zombies that attacked the village were just random shamblers who came down off the mountain," Curtis said, ticking off points one by one on the fingers of one hand, "and it was just a coincidence that two hordes attacked us in those ruins at the same time, and there's been a rise in undead activity in the northern part of the country because fate is a fickle bitch and we're just that unlucky, not because there is some grand plan at work being masterminded by some evil genius up in the mountains. Does that sound about right to you guys?"

"That just about covers it, I think," Sergeant Josiah answered quietly.

"I knew it!" Curtis threw his hands in the air. "Whole thing was just a waste of our damned time."

"Oh," Sibyl said from the far side of the room, "I think it might well be a little worse than a waste of time, I'm afraid. A good deal worse, in fact."

Jun turned to look in her direction, and saw that the Englishwoman was standing beneath the bank of screens that lined the far wall.

"These show the hallways we just passed through," Sibyl said, pointing to the screens on the bottom row. Even from her vantage point across the room Jun could see movement on the screens, and as she crossed the floor to stand beside Sibyl she could clearly make out several of the Dead making their shambling way down the corridor. Then Sibyl pointed to the top row of screens. "And *these* show the hangar through which we entered."

Jun raised her gaze to look at the top screens. The one on the top left showed the interior of the hangar from a point somewhere high on the outer wall, and as Jun watched several of the Dead made their way into the hangar from the doorway that lead to the interior corridor beyond. Another screen displayed the reverse view, showing the rolling hangar doors that lead outside. On that screen, Jun watched as several more of the Dead were leaving the hangar and moving out onto the landing pad, passing through the three-foot gap left below the bottom edge of the hangar door. The squad had left the rolling doors open when they entered the facility, in case they needed to make a hasty exit. It would never have occurred to Jun that something else might exit the fortress by that route, instead.

"They're getting out," Sibyl went on, sounding mournful. "They've been locked down here in the dark all of this time, with no way out, and then we came along and opened all of the locked doors barring their way."

Jun's eyes darted to the other screens. She saw the barracks they had passed, and the hundreds of Dead who were pouring out of the open doors into the corridors beyond. And the screens showing the hundreds upon hundreds of the Dead who shambled and jostled through the hallways and corridors of the fortress. Even now they were beginning to spill out of the hallways into the stairs leading to the upper levels, and it was only a matter of time before they all made their way to the hangar and out into the open air beyond.

"There's..." Curtis began and faltered, all composure lost, his eyes wide and his mouth hanging open, without a trace of his customary cynical detachment. "There's so *many*…"

"A whole goddamned army of the bastards," Josiah said in a low voice.

Jun couldn't bring herself to speak, her thoughts racing as she processed what they were seeing. The sergeant was correct, it was an entire army of the Dead, and thanks to the actions of Jun and the rest of their squad, it would now be unleashed on an unsuspecting world. The reanimated remains of the SS officers and Hitler youth who had been sent to the Alpine Redoubt in the last days before Plan Z was carried out would in a sense complete their original mission. They had been sent up into the Alps to wait for the coming day when they would wage war on their enemies in the lowlands below. And now they would, making their mindless way down the mountains in search of heat and life, destroying and consuming all who had the misfortune to be in their path.

The forces of the Resistance in Northern Italy were already strained to the breaking point, hardly able to deal with a relatively minor increase in Dead activity in recent weeks. How could they hope to withstand the hundreds upon hundreds of the Dead who would now be descending upon them? How long until the whole of Reclamation Zone Italia was affected? The Resistance forces would doubtless be able to overcome eventually, but how many would die needlessly in the meantime, both Resistance fighters and civilians alike?

"What...?" Curtis turned in a slow circle, his gaze passing over each of their faces in turn until finally coming to rest on the sergeant's. "What are we going to *do*?"

"They can't get through that door, clearly," Sibyl said, nodding in the direction of the reinforced door through which they'd entered the control center. "We could wait them out, let their numbers thin a bit, and then fight our way to freedom."

The young American wheeled on the Englishwoman, his eyes wide with shock. "What, and just let the undead bastards loose on the world?"

Sibyl's expression was carefully guarded, her jaw clenched and her lips pressed tightly together.

"An untold number of the Dead already roam the countryside," she said, "and their ranks being increased by these unfortunates would mean a difference of degree, not of kind."

"Tell that to the people who are gonna get themselves eaten by the goddamned zombies we just turned loose," Curtis said, his cheeks flushing red with emotion.

Sibyl's eyes flashed darkly, and an unfamiliar expression settled over her normally composed features. It seemed to Jun as if the stiff-upper-lip calm composure that the older Englishwoman normally projected to the world was like a mask that she wore, and that mask was beginning to slip. Because Sibyl suddenly looked jaded and world-weary, and tired of it all.

"We all die in the end, dear boy," she said with no trace of warm or humor. "Cancer takes us, or a truck runs us over, and we die needless in some godforsaken war in some godforsaken desert far from our homes and the ones who love us." Her eyes darted for the briefest of instants to Werner, and then back to Curtis. "We cannot hope to defeat death, only delay the inevitable."

Curtis looked shocked, and it was clear that he was not quite as cynical as he liked to let on.

"No, enough of that," Sergeant Josiah said, cutting off the response that Curtis was clearly about to deliver, silencing the both of them with a wave of his hand. "There ain't nobody else but us who can do anything about this mess, y'all, so we're going to fix it."

The sergeant drew his Colt M1911 semiautomatic from the holster at his hip, and started towards the door.

"We're going to fix it, dammit," he repeated, "or die trying."

CHAPTER 22

ONLY A MATTER of moments had gone by since Jun and the others had entered the command center through that reinforced door, but now that they were about to exit through that same door everything had changed. No longer were they hoping to find the supposed mastermind of the Alpine Fortress with some faint hope of surviving long enough to escape back to the outside. Now they had to fight their way through the zombie hordes roaming the hallways of the facility in time to keep the army of the Dead from spilling out and threatening countless lives beyond the walls of the fortress.

But at the very least, Jun thought as she tried to find some upside, they no longer had to worry about stealth or subtlety.

"Everybody locked and loaded and ready to roll out?" Sergeant Josiah had one hand on the door handle, the other holding his Colt M1911 at the ready.

"Ready as I'll ever be," Curtis drawled in response.

"What are our orders, sir?" Jun asked, tightening her grip on the stock of her submachine gun.

"Put the bastards down and try not to get killed your ownself," Josiah replied.

"That has a certain elegant simplicity, I'd say," Sibyl chimed in.

"But seriously," the sergeant continued, glancing back over his shoulder at Jun after hearing her weary sigh, "we're going to drive right through the middle of the bastards in a tight vanguard, just like we did on our way to base camp, heading in the direction of the stairs to the upper levels. Any of the Dead bastards who we leave behind still standing aren't any concern of ours. Our only worry should be the Dead who are *ahead* of us, and getting up to that hangar on the top level before too many of them get through the hangar doors. So, your orders basically are…"

"Put the bastards down," Jun replied, "and try not to get killed ourselves."

Josiah flashed her a quick smile, and winked, before turning his attention back to the door.

"Werner, are we good?" the sergeant called back

to the German soldier, who was glaring daggers
at the corpse of the dead Waffen-SS colonel in the
swivel chair. "Can we count on you to show up to
work here?"

Werner spared one last angry glance at Ziegler's
body, then blinked hard and turned back to face
the sergeant. "I am here, Herr Sergeant. You may
rely on me."

"Glad to hear it. Okay, y'all, good luck out there.
Now let's roll out."

With that, the sergeant turned the handle and
then leaned forward, driving his shoulder into the
door to shove it open. The door almost immediately
hit something on the other side, partially arresting
its motion, and the head and shoulders of one of the
Dead lurched into view in the gap.

Josiah didn't pause an instant, but raised his Colt
and fired a round point blank that hit the Dead
right in its forehead. As the lifeless body collapsed
to the floor, the sergeant shoved the door once
more with his shoulder, and it banged open against
the wall on the other side.

Werner and Jun immediately stepped in front
of the sergeant, providing cover for him as he
holstered his Colt and unslung his pump-action
shotgun from his shoulder. Werner took aim with
his Karabiner and fired a round at another of the

Dead shambling towards the door, and Jun took out another with her submachine gun, while the sergeant worked the pump to chamber a round in his shotgun. Werner and Jun took up positions on either side of the door outside, drawing a bead and firing again and again.

Sibyl and Curtis followed the sergeant out into the hallway while Werner and Jun continued to lay down suppressing fire. The squad was now in a roughly box-shaped formation, with the sergeant in the middle flanked front and back by the other members of the squad.

The Dead jostled and shambled erratically through the hallways, but aside from the few who had pursued the squad through the corridor to the command center in the first place and then lingered waiting for them on the other side of the door, the rest of them seemed only now to be becoming aware of the squad's location. Whether attracted by their body heat or some kind of life energy or whatever answer one could formulate for what motivated the undead, the zombies were reacting to the squad's arrival in the hallway, and moving to intercept them from all directions.

Which meant, Jun realized, that not only would the squad need to contend with the Dead who lay between them and their objective, but they would also need to be wary of Dead who would be *following* them.

"Forward," the sergeant shouted as he moved up to a point a half-pace ahead of Sibyl and Curtis, who fell into position on his flank to either side. Jun and Werner followed suit, taking their places to either side of the inverted-V formation.

"Clear a path!" Sergeant Josiah blasted a zombie who was shambling towards him, and then immediately stepped over the body that fell on the floor at his feet, moving closer to the intersection of corridors up ahead.

With the voice of the dead colonel no longer droning on from the now-silent loudspeakers overhead, the hallway now was filled with the shuffling footsteps of the Dead, their inhuman shrieks, and the constant chorus of the squad's weapons firing again and again and again. The clamorous din was near deafening, and Jun found it more than a little disorienting. It brought to mind the tumult surrounding the defense of the embassy in Moscow when the Dead first rose: the shouts of the city's defenders, the screams of the terrified citizenry, the shrieks of the invading undead hordes. Jun bit back the anxiety and fear she could feel welling up from deep within, and instead focused on the anger that those memories brought with them, and vented her rage on the Dead surrounding her, firing round after round from her Thompson into the oncoming swell.

They were making decent progress by the time they reached the intersection where several corridors met, and it was only after glancing back the way that they'd come that Jun saw that the command center door was still only a dozen or so paces away. She was in the process of replacing the magazine drum of her submachine gun when she realized that the sergeant had brought the squad to a halt, with Dead closing in from all sides.

"God *DAMN* it," the sergeant muttered. "Which way is it…?"

Jun glanced back over her shoulder in his direction, and immediately recognized the trouble. In the confusion of their hasty advance through the facility to the command center in the first place, following the course of the cabling from the surveillance cameras overhead, they were now having to retrace their steps but without the benefit of any familiar landmarks, since the cabling that came together at the junction box above the command center door now branched off in all directions the farther they went. Which evidently now left the sergeant unsure which of the branching corridors to follow.

Fortunately, Jun had spent more time facing back the way they'd come as she brought up the rear and fended off the encroaching Dead while Sibyl inspected the door's lock, and knew exactly which hallway it was that they'd come down.

"Second on the left!" Jun shouted back over her shoulder, punctuating her words with a burst of fire from her Thompson M1A1, dropping a zombie who was almost within arm's reach.

"Copy that!" Josiah replied, and motioned for the squad to move in that direction. "Move out!"

Once they'd made it through the scrum of Dead that crowded the intersection and through to the corridor that Jun had indicated, the going became relatively easier. It appeared that with Dead converging on their position outside the command center from all sides, the growing horde had formed a bottleneck of sorts in the intersection, limiting both the number of Dead that the squad had left to encounter as they charge towards the stairway at the far end of the hallway, as well as cutting down on the number of Dead who were able to pursue them from behind.

Few of the Dead were able to keep pace with them so long as the squad kept moving at a healthy clip, and so Jun felt a tremor of optimism as the door to the stairway came into view before them, with only a handful of the Dead between the squad and their goal.

Then that brief tremor immediately subsided into stark pessimism when a partially-open side door burst wide open just as the squad passed by, and a small horde of zombies rushed out towards them from only a few feet away.

"Bastard!" Curtis shouted as one of the Dead grabbed hold of his left arm, dragged him close, and immediately sunk its teeth into the meat of his left shoulder. The young American tried to fire a round from his M1 Carbine, but the shot went wide as his face was twisted in a rictus of pain and terror.

Sibyl reacted immediately, instinctually, rushing forward and bashing the zombie in the face with the butt of her Lee Enfield, hitting it hard enough to smash its nose into paste and knock loose one of its eyeballs from its socket. The zombie released its bite on Curtis's shoulder, and as it reared back and prepared to attack Sibyl instead, she spun her rifle around and fired a round from the hip that exploded up and through the zombie's skull, sending a shower of gore flying into the air.

Curtis was bent forward, gripping his left shoulder with his right hand as blood welled freely through his fingers. Sibyl bent down and picked up

Curtis's Carbine from the floor, then slung it over her shoulder as she moved to his side and helped him stand up straight.

"Come along, dear," Sibyl said, the plummy tones of her voice only slightly showing the strain and stress of the moment, "mustn't dawdle. We're all in this together."

With Curtis's arm around her shoulder for support, Sibyl fired another round in the mass of Dead issuing forth from the side door.

"A little more haste might be in order, Josiah," she called over her shoulder back to the sergeant, who was busy blasting away at the Dead himself.

"We're almost there, sir!" Jun shouted, scanning the route ahead. There were now only two or three of the Dead between them and the stairway door. If they were able to move quickly past the horde that had emerged from the side door, and quickly put down the few who remained in their way, then they would be able to reach the stairs without much difficulty. Assuming of course that no more surprises lay in store for them.

Jun wasn't sure they would be so lucky.

The sergeant and the others were still fending off the newcomers who were crowding out of the side door towards them, which Jun now realized must lead to one of the barracks that they'd passed on their way in. So Jun, in an uncharacteristic moment, opted not to wait for orders but to make an executive decision on her own. Leaving her position on the rear flank, she stepped forward past the others and focused her fire on the Dead shambling towards them from the front. Three bodies dropped one after another as her shots hit home. Then she raced forward, covering the short distance that remained, and skidded to a stop just in front of the door to the stairway.

Like all of the doors that they had opened and unlocked as they made their way deeper into the fortress, it was still unlocked and partially ajar. Raising her submachine gun, Jun nudged the bottom of the door with her foot and then peered through the open gap into the stairway beyond. The steps leading up appeared to be clear of the Dead, though she could hear movement from somewhere above.

"Come on, this way!" Jun shouted back down the hallway, slinging her submachine gun over her shoulder and switching to her T-99 instead. She took careful aim through the rifle's scope, and then began squeezing off shots and picking off the Dead menacing the rest of the squad one by one. "Door's open and the stairs are clear!"

Sibyl and Curtis reached the stairs first, with the young American leaning heavily on the

Englishwoman for support, his shoulder and left side stained darkly with his own blood. Josiah and Werner followed close behind, walking backwards down the hallway as they fired their weapons back the way that they'd come, keeping the pursuing Dead from overtaking them.

Jun held the door open as first Sibyl and Curtis and then Werner and Josiah passed through. When the whole squad was in the stairway, Jun slammed the door shut, and then looked in vain for a way to bar or bolt the door.

"Can you make this locked again, Sibyl?" Jun asked urgently, as she could hear the Dead approaching from the other side.

"I learned the trick to *unlocking* doors, dear," Sibyl replied with weary humor, straining slightly under the weight of the injured Curtis, "but never tried my hand at using my picks to *lock* one. It's possible, I suppose, but…"

"We don't have that kind of time," Josiah cut in, already starting up the steps to the next floor. "Our concern is what's ahead, remember, not what's behind."

And as the squad trooped up the brightly-lit steps to the next level, it felt to Jun as though they were climbing up out of the tomb, leaving behind the stale air and gloomy unease of the lower level for the light and stillness of the levels above. But she was mindful that many of the Dead had already left the tomb ahead of them, and that the stillness and light that they'd passed through on the squad's way down might not be there to greet them on the way back out…

CHAPTER 23

THERE WERE ALREADY a number of the Dead roaming the next level up when they exited the stairwell, and by that point Jun could already hear the sounds of more of them coming up the stairs from below.

"Damn, it didn't take them long to get that open," Josiah said, casting a quick glance over his shoulder back down the way they'd come. "Hopefully the stairs'll slow 'em down a little."

Curtis was in a bad way, able to maintain his footing with Sibyl's help but not much more than that. His left arm hung useless at his side, while his right hand was occupied trying to stem the flow of blood from the gaping wound in his shoulder. Sibyl was unable to work the bolt on her Lee Enfield with one arm helping to keep Curtis on his feet, and so was limited to using her revolver to keep the Dead ahead at bay. So the squad had to adapt to a new marching order. With Josiah in the lead and Werner and Jun at his flanks, they began to drive down the hallway towards the final set of stairs at the far end, with Sibyl and Curtis following close behind.

Most of the Dead who had reached this level ahead of them and hadn't already moved on to the top level were crowded at the far end of the hallway, jostling against one another as they attempted to make their way through the stairway to the upper level and the hangar beyond. A half-dozen or so stragglers had noted the arrival of the squad from the floor beneath them, and turned back to shamble in their direction.

Jun didn't need to wait for orders this time, and she raised her T-99 as both the sergeant and Werner leveled their own rifles and took aim.

Three shots sounded out like peals of thunder, as the rearmost of the shambling Dead ahead of them toppled to the floor, rotten grey matter and ichor-like blood geysering up from their exploding skulls. Then three more shots a split second later after they'd chambered another round, and another trio of the Dead were collapsing to the floor in motionless heaps.

Having taken account of the six zombies who were already shambling back in their direction, the sergeant motioned the squad to advance. And so he, Jun, and Werner took two paces forward, took aim and fired, then another two paces as they chambered another round in their rifles, then drew a bead and fired again, and so on as they continued down the corridor.

By the time the squad closed the distance between them and the stairway leading to the top level, all of the zombies in the corridor were down, rotting corpses strewn all over the floor in their wake. Jun allowed herself to entertain the notion that the worst of it might be behind them. Then they stepped into the stairway and that notion was long gone.

The zombies were slower going up steps that they were shambling across a level floor, and so even as slow as their forward progress typically was there had been a gradual buildup as the Dead entering the stairs run up against those who were already making their slow way up the steps. And so, now that the squad had caught up, they found a veritable unbroken wall of undead flesh before them, with dozens upon dozens of the Dead crammed into the dozen or so steps from where they now stood to the next landing up ahead.

"Forget this nonsense," the sergeant snarled as he raised the barrel of his 12-gauge shotgun and let off a blast into the nearest of the Dead.

Jun switched to her submachine gun and Werner to his MP40 as the two of them squeezed into the stairwell on either side of the sergeant and unloaded their clips into the wall of unliving bodies on the steps above. There was no time now for careful aim and precision. This was wholesale slaughter, mechanized death with an unending hail of gunfire, the Dead being mown down like wheat before the scythe.

She reloaded her Thompson as she climbed over the lower rows of the fallen, and continued firing on the Dead above. The bodies of the fallen Dead were so thick that her feet didn't even touch the floor, and instead she was scrambling over their rotting corpses like a mountain goat over unsteady terrain.

"Make haste, friends!" Sibyl called from a short distance behind, and Jun glanced back to see the Englishwoman aiming her Lee Enfield and firing back down the hallway the way they'd come, while Curtis leaned against the wall, all color drained from his cheeks and his eyes half-lidded.

From her vantage halfway up to the next landing, Jun could see that the zombies who had followed them from the floor below were beginning to catch up, and had almost reached the bottom of the stairs. Unless the squad speeded their advance up the stairs, they ran the risk of being pincered between the Dead before them and behind.

But Curtis seemed unlikely to climb the mound of bodies that littered the stairs without assistance, and Sibyl was too busy fending off the Dead who were approaching down the hallway to help him up.

"Curtis!" Jun shouted as she turned and hopped over the bodies on the steps to reach the bottom of the stairs. She put one arm around Curtis's back and pulled him towards her. "Let's go!"

Then with Jun practically shouldering Curtis's entire weight, the two of them slowly made their way up the bottom steps, climbing over the fallen Dead while Sibyl fired round after round from her Lee Enfield at the zombies closing in on them from behind.

"Come on!" the sergeant shouted from the landing above. "The rest of the way is clear!"

Jun had almost helped Curtis all the way to the landing where Werner was now standing when she heard a deafening scream from behind. She turned back, and saw that Sibyl was staggering backwards. One of the Dead had barreled into her, wrapping its bony arms around her legs, and was in the process of taking an enormous bite out of her thigh.

"Sibyl!" Jun shouted as she immediately raised her Thompson and fired it one handed without even having a chance to aim. Her bullets tore into the back of the zombie that had knocked Sibyl down, but it continued gnawing on her thigh.

Werner rushed past Jun, diving down the stairs and pulling a combat knife from a sheath at his belt. In one fluid motion he brought the point of the blade down and buried it in the side of the zombie's skull, then wrenched its now-motionless jaws off of Sibyl's leg.

"Here, Frau Beaton, allow me," Werner said, taking hold of Sibyl's hand and helping her to her feet. She was unable to put any weight on her injured leg, and Werner as much as held her up. For her part, Sibyl was so stricken by pain and shock that she could do little but mutter an unending series of curses beneath her breath, displaying a breadth and scope of vulgarity that Jun was shocked to learn the Englishwoman possessed.

With the sergeant and Jun providing cover fire from above, Werner half-carried, half-helped Sibyl up the pile of bodies to the landing, and then up the stairs to the upper level. Then the sergeant assisted Curtis up to the top while Jun laid down suppressing fire on any pursuers.

Finally all five members of the squad were on

the upper level of the fortress, albeit a little worse for wear. It seemed to Jun that Sibyl's injuries might even be worse than the ones that Curtis had sustained, and it was clear that neither of them would be able simply to tie a bandana around their wounds and soldier on, as she herself had, what seemed like a lifetime ago. The cut that she had gotten climbing out of the electrical conduit had been the barest of scratches compared to the gaping, freely-bleeding holes in her two squad mates.

But they didn't have any time to pause and tend to their wounds. The zombies from below were still at their heels, and they still had to make their way to the hangar and close the main doors.

"Remember, our concern is what's ahead of us, y'all," the sergeant reiterated, sounding even wearier than before, "not what's behind. Let's keep moving."

There were only a bare handful of the Dead roaming this upper level, and it was a matter of relative ease to pot them with headshots from a distance, clearing the squad's way to the entrance to the hangar at the far end of the corridor. If not for the fact that two of her squad mates were in the process of bleeding to death and a horde of ravenous zombies were following close behind,

Jun would have been tempted to think that things were working out in their favor.

Then they reached the hangar. And if reaching the stairway crammed with the Dead moments before had put paid to the notion that the worst of it was behind them, seeing what lay before them in the hangar demolished the idea that anything at all might be working out in their favor.

The hangar was overrun with the Dead.

"Aw, hell," Josiah said, shoulders slumping.

From wall to wall the space was crawling with zombies, that ebbed and flowed like the tides. On the far side of the hangar Jun could see them streaming out beneath the open hangar door in dribs and drabs, into the bright early morning light beyond. But there were still more of the Dead milling around the midst of the hangar than they had encountered so far in the fortress put together. One of the barracks that they'd opened up on their initial descent into the fortress must have housed more of the Dead than they'd realized, and the damned things had been streaming their way up here to the hangar nearly the entire time that the squad had been downstairs.

Jun's eyes scouted the way ahead, and through the milling horde she saw the doorway to the control room on the far right wall, where she had found the controls that opened the main rolling hangar door. Thankfully, she had closed the control room door behind her, and through the leaded windows she could see that there were no zombies inside the small space. But to reach the control room they would have to carve their way through the horde before them.

"Over there!" she shouted, grabbing hold of the sergeant's elbow to get his attention, and pointed in the direction of the control room door. "We need to get in there!"

"Copy that," Josiah answered, immediately regaining his focus. "Lead the way, kid."

It was a distance that, without obstruction or obstacle, they could cover in the span of a dozen or so paces. But with the milling Dead blocking their way, the going was considerably more time-consuming and arduous. Jun was conscious of the fact that she only had one more full drum magazine on her, and so was more judicious with her shots from the Thompson than she had been back in the stairwell. But still she fired almost constantly, aiming for the heads of the zombies that milled in their path, dropping them like flies one after another.

"Keep at it!" the sergeant urged from behind her. Jun didn't turn around or even acknowledge the encouragement, but rammed the last magazine into place and continued firing into the crowd.

But so focused was she on the obstacles directly before her that she was hardly aware of the progress they were making, and as a result she was surprised when one of the Dead toppled in front of her and she saw the control room door immediately behind where it had fallen.

"Cover me!" she called back over her shoulder, then stepped over the fallen Dead and took hold of the door handle. It turned easily in her grip, and she stepped aside to provide cover fire while the sergeant helped Curtis stumble through, and then came Werner carrying Sibyl. Jun fired the last rounds from her submachine gun, clearing just enough of a space around the control room door to give her time to slip inside and close the door behind her.

Jun was catching her breath as she heard the clanking of the chain-and-pulley system grinding to life and beginning to winch the rolling door shut, but then the sound ceased almost before it had begun.

"God *DAMN* it," she could hear the sergeant muttering.

"What?" Jun turned away from the door and looked over to the bank of controls where the sergeant and Werner were standing, while Sibyl and Curtis leaned limply against the back wall.

The sergeant had his hand hovering above the lever marked with the German words for "door" and "open," a scowl on his face. He pressed the lever, and the door mechanism ground to life once more, but the second he lifted his hand the lever snapped back into the off position and the door stopped moving.

"The system is manual, it only works when someone is turning the key," Josiah said, eyes low to the ground. "If we're going to get out of here, someone is going to have to stay behind and close the door behind us."

CHAPTER 24

"WELL, STOP PLAYING silly buggers," Sibyl said, her voice strained and breathless. "It's obvious who needs to stick around, isn't it?"

Jun and the others turned and glanced over to where the Englishwoman was leaning against the wall of the control room, looking even more pale and unsteady than she had just a moment before.

"I mean, how am I meant to climb down a bloody mountain with *this*?" Sibyl asked, gesturing to the generous wound on her thigh. "I can barely stand up as it is. So stick me in a chair, point me at the lever, and let's get on with it already."

Before Jun or any of the others could react, Curtis cut in.

"I'm in a bad way, folks," the young American said, sounding like he was having trouble maintaining consciousness, much less focus or alertness, "and I've been bleeding out a whole lot longer than Missus Beaton here. You should take her with you down the mountain, and leave *me* to take care of this."

"Stuff and nonsense," Sibyl shot back, starting to gesture in Curtis' direction and then almost losing her balance entirely. Werner rushed to her side and took hold of her arm just before she fell backwards onto the floor.

"Damn it, y'all," the sergeant muttered under his breath. Jun could see that he was struggling with the choice, and deeply unhappy that any of them had to be left behind, and even less so that ultimately the decision of who it was to be fell to him.

"I think that…" Werner began, but then was cut off when the interior of the control room was filled with the sound of shattering glass.

Jun spun around, and saw that the zombies on the other side of the door had smashed through one of the windows, despite the wires reinforcing the leaded glass. And while they were so far just reaching cadaverous arms through the gap, bony hands grasping and scrambling like skeletal spiders, rotting flesh torn away by the jagged edges of broken glass, it would only be a matter of time before one of them crawled bodily through all the way.

"We don't have time for this," Curtis said, and raised his semi-automatic pistol in a blood-slicked fist, firing a round at one of the Dead flailing through the broken window. "Mrs. Beaton, get on that lever, and I'll keep them off your back. The rest of you get out of here!"

There was no more time for debate or delay. If they didn't move quickly, they would be trapped in the control room.

The sergeant nodded once in Curtis's direction, and then moved a rolling chair into place in front of the lever while Werner helped Sibyl cross the floor. Then Jun and the sergeant helped Sibyl lower herself down onto the seat of the chair, wincing in pain and discomfort as she did.

"Good luck," the sergeant said simply, laying a hand on Sibyl's shoulder, and then moved to the door, firing a shotgun blast through the broken window as he went.

Jun lingered for a moment by Sibyl's side. She could not help remembering the moment when she had been forced to watch her friends swallowed up by a ravening horde in Moscow, and now she felt like she was back in the exact same position once again.

Sibyl looked up and met Jun's gaze, and blinked slowly before answering.

"Make it... count," the Englishwoman managed to get out with some difficulty. There were flecks of blood at the corners of her mouth, and Jun realized that the extent of Sibyl's injuries were even greater than she had realized.

Jun squeezed Sibyl's hand once, lips pressed tightly together, and then rushed over to join Josiah and Werner by the door.

"Y'all ready?" Josiah asked them both, his hand on the door knob.

"Give the word, Herr Sergeant," Werner replied.

Jun chanced a quick glance over to Sibyl in the chair, her hand poised over the door control lever, with Curtis standing directly behind her, bracing himself against the wall and firing round after round at the zombies attempting to claw their way through the broken window and into the control room.

"Well, kid?" the sergeant added, nudging Jun with his elbow. "You with us?"

She turned back and met his gaze, then nodded. "Let's go."

"Alright, then," Josiah said, and yanked the door open with one swift move, immediately stepping aside so Werner and Jun had a clear line of fire to shoot through the doorway.

In the blink of an eye the three of them were on

the other side, and the sergeant was slamming the door shut behind them.

"Don't let up!" Josiah shouted, firing a round from his 12-gauge into the face of a zombie lurching towards him, racking the pump and then firing at another.

As she had used up the last drum magazine for her Thompson submachine gun, Jun's choices were limited to her T-99 rifle and her Webley revolver. With the Dead in such close quarters, she opted for the Webley as they drove their way through the crowd and towards the hangar door.

When they were maybe a dozen paces from the door, Jun could hear the sound of the chain-and-pulley mechanism clanking to life, and looking ahead she could see that the rolling door was slowly beginning to close. She, Josiah, and Werner would reach the door in time to get under and out before it shut, but it would be cutting it close. They needed some small advantage, something that would occupy the shambling horde even for a brief moment. Because besides the ones who were still trying to smash the remaining windows and climb into the control room, the rest of the Dead jostling around the hangar had turned their attention to the three squad mates fighting their way towards the exit.

They still had a half-dozen hard-fought steps to go until they reached the door when Jun remembered the drums of gasoline that she had spotted on the far wall of the hangar when she had first looked out from the grill of the electrical conduit. Without sparing a breath to tell Josiah or Werner about her plan, she decided to improvise, and taking hold of her T-99 swung its barrel around, peered through the telescopic sight and took aim, and squeezed off a round at the bottommost of the petrol tanks.

First one and then all of the barrels erupted in a massive explosion that ripped through the far side of the hangar. Dozens of the Dead were caught in the swiftly expanding fireball, their inhuman shrieks sounding out as the flames consumed them.

The Dead closest to the corner of the hangar where Jun and the others were fighting through were not directly caught in the blast, but with the pressure of those now-burning corpses no longer pushing from behind, the leading edge of the horde had lost some of its forward moment. And with a final surge of speed Jun burst through the crowd and dove beneath the hangar door, thankful that the chain-and-pulleys had ceased moving just before she slid under.

For the briefest of instants Jun worried that the Dead had overrun the control room and that Sibyl was no longer able to man the door controls, but as soon as Josiah and Werner slipped out underneath the bottom edge of the door, the chain-and-pulleys once more clanked to life and the rolling door slammed shut in a matter of seconds.

Sibyl had halted the door's closing just long enough to let them out, and then closed it the rest of the way as soon as they were clear.

"Gott im Himmel," Werner swore under his breath.

There were a few grasping limbs that stuck out beneath the bottom of the door, and at least one of the Dead had been decapitated when the door closed on its neck, but otherwise the door had completely shut and there was no way for any of the Dead within to get out now.

Of course, there were the Dead who had already gotten out still to worry about.

Jun was bent over with her hands on her knees, struggling to catch her breath. Turning her head to look across the landing pad, Jun could see a handful of the Dead still shambling across the pavement, no doubt following those who had descended the mountain ahead of them. There was no way of knowing how many of the Dead had already made it out of the hangar and were even now on their way towards the populated areas at the base of the mountains.

It was clear that the sergeant was thinking along similar lines.

"We'll need to catch up with them as already headed down the mountain," he said, sounding weary.

Werner was in the process of reloading his MP40, a stoic silence settling over him, but Jun could see a pained look in his eyes.

Jun straightened up and looked back at the hangar door. The sound of the Dead within could be faintly heard through the reinforced metal door, along with the distant peals of Curtis's pistol firing. There was a brief silence, and then another shot rang out, immediately followed by another, and then only the muffled sounds of the writhing Dead horde could be heard.

"Oh…" Jun covered her mouth with her hand as she realized what those final two gunshots meant, and who had taken each of the last two bullets.

Sergeant Josiah stepped over to Jun's side, and laid a hand on her shoulder.

"Come on, kid," he said softly. Jun could hear his voice almost break, but Josiah maintained his composure. "Remember, we've got to concern ourselves with what's ahead of us, not what's behind."

Sibyl had told her that she needed to make it count. Jun owed it to her, and to Curtis, and to her fallen friends and all of the others who had gone ahead of them, to keep moving. To aim for the head, scan for incoming, and keep moving.

"Okay," Jun said, and began reloading her Webley. "Let's go make it count."

And as the sun raised over the peaks of the Alps that loomed in the east, the three survivors began to make their way down the mountain, leaving the fortress of the Dead behind them, to carry on the fight against the armies of the unliving.

Jun would make it count, for the sake of all those who had gone before her, or die trying...

ABOUT THE AUTHOR

CHRIS ROBERSON IS the co-creator with artist Michael Allred of *iZombie*, the basis of the hit CW television series, and the writer of several New York Times best-selling *Cinderella* miniseries set in the world of Bill Willingham's *Fables*. He is also the co-creator of *Edison Rex* with artist Dennis Culver, and the co-writer of *Hellboy and the B.P.R.D, Witchfinder, Rise of the Black Flame*, and other titles set in the world of Mike Mignola's *Hellboy*. In addition to his numerous comics projects, Roberson has written more than a dozen novels and three dozen short stories.

FIND US ONLINE!

www.rebellionpublishing.com

/rebellionpub   /rebellionpublishing   /rebellionpub

SIGN UP TO OUR NEWSLETTER!

rebellionpublishing.com/sign-up

YOUR REVIEWS MATTER!

Enjoy this book? Got something to say?

Leave a review on Amazon, GoodReads or with your
favourite bookseller and let the world know!

THE COMPLETE

DOUBLE DEAD

NEW YORK TIMES BEST SELLING AUTHOR OF *STAR WARS: AFTERMATH*

CHUCK WENDIG

"Wendig is ferociously inventive and effortlessly sharp"
Richard Dansky, author of *Beloved of the Dead* and *Firefly Rain*

ISBN (UK): 978-1-781084-20-5 (US): 978-1-781084-20-5
UK £12.99   US $16.99   CAN $18.99